Elspeth Sandys

Timaru-born author Elspeth Sandys has had a dual career as an actress and a successful novelist and playwright. From Auckland's Mercury Theatre Company, Elspeth travelled to England to continue her acting career in radio and television. After the birth of her two children she began writing for the BBC and had many of her radio plays broadcast, in addition to publishing a string of successful novels and a collection of short stories. Her novel *Riverlines* was a finalist for the UK Orange Prize in 1996. After 21 years in England, Elspeth Sandys returned to New Zealand in 1990. *A Passing Guest* is her eighth novel.

CW01560377

ORIGINAL

A PASSING GUEST

ELSPETH SANDYS

Flamingo
An imprint of HarperCollins*Publishers*

Published with the assistance of a grant from creative nz
ARTS COUNCIL OF NEW ZEALAND TOI AOTEAROA

National Library of New Zealand Cataloguing-in-Publication Data

Sandys, Elspeth.
A passing guest / Elspeth Sandys.
ISBN 1-86950-405-4
1. New Zealand fiction-21st century. I. Title.
NZ823.2-dc 21

Flamingo
An imprint of HarperCollins*Publishers*

First published 2002
HarperCollins*Publishers (New Zealand) Limited*
P.O. Box 1, Auckland

ISBN 1 86950 405 4

Set in Aldine 401
Designed and typeset by Chris O'Brien/Pages LP
Printed by Griffin Press, Australia on 80 gsm Econoprint

I am a passing guest, as all my forefathers were.

Psalm 39

The only time I know something is true is at the moment I discover it in the act of writing.

Jean Malaquais

. . . have patience with everything unresolved in your heart and try to love the questions themselves . . .
Don't search for the answers, which could not be given to you now, because you would not be able to live them. And the point is, to live everything. Live the questions now. Perhaps then, someday far in the future, you will gradually, without even noticing it, live your way into the answer.

Rainer Maria Rilke

Tout comprendre, c'est tout pardonner.

French proverb

In memory of Ben

Acknowledgements

My largest debt is to my daughter, Josie Harbutt, whose insight and courage inspired me to write this story.

Thanks are due also to Judge Oke Blaikie and Glen Houghton, who advised me on legal matters; to Dr John Lusk, whose advice I sought on medical issues; to Roy and Jeanette Walker who surfed the internet for me; to Dr Ralph Crane, who read the text in manuscript form, and made a number of helpful suggestions; and to Des Foulger, whose computer expertise kept me sane and working. To Juliet Batten and Jude Meikle, warm thanks for their faith and encouragement.

The following books proved invaluable in my research: *Redemption Songs* by Judith Binney; *Staunch* by Bill Payne; *Hui* by Anne Salmond.

The first draft of *A Passing Guest* was written while I was Writer-in-Residence at the University of Waikato. I would like to thank that University, and Creative New Zealand, for their support.

1

'What are you doing here?' I ask.

'What are *you*?' Pete answers.

I look around me, a lingering look while I think what to say. I take in the mountain with its irregular lines of terraces; the road that will take me back to the city; the small stone church built by settlers; the hibiscus trees shrouded with dying flowers; the headstones with names in Maori, Samoan, Rarotongan. Finally I take in Pete's face, streaked with pain; his hurt, enquiring eyes.

I say, 'I'm here for the same thing you are. To find answers.'

I dreamed of Max last night. He stood unsmiling at the end of my bed, and said in words as clear as a morepork's cry: 'I'm OK, Renate. No one hassles me here. I'm getting sorted.'

I woke in a sweat. '*You're* getting sorted,' I raged. 'What about me?'

'OK,' Pete says, after we've sat in silence for a while. 'You're the one with the words.'

'It's beautiful here,' I comment.

'The country of the dead,' Pete reminds me.

'That isn't why it's beautiful, is it?'

Pete shrugs. I've seen that closed look on his face before, usually when he's engaged in the struggle to breathe. Pete is asthmatic. But it's not asthma that's troubling him today.

'Max's death wasn't . . .' I don't really know what I'm trying to say. Something to comfort. 'You know . . .' I finish lamely.

'No, I don't know,' Pete answers fiercely. 'I don't know why it happened. Why did it have to . . .'

'Maybe . . .' I struggle with a thought I haven't dared give voice to before. Pete and his sister Lily are the ones I feel closest to in Max's family. Yet they can go opaque on me when they choose. They can make me feel an outsider. 'Maybe it was his gift to us,' I hazard.

I wonder for a moment if Pete's heard me. His plump, clean-shaven face, which Max once described as the face of a Maori monk, stays locked in the frown he's worn since my arrival. He scoops up a pile of dirt, and scatters it over the grass. I have the feeling he wants to dig Max up — interrogate him, as we had neglected to do when he was alive. 'Not a gift,' he says. 'Something though. Dunno what.'

You're right, I think, a gift would make things too easy. And nothing about Max was ever easy.

Pete is Max's youngest brother. I don't know his age exactly, but he can't be more than twenty-four or five. Max's family has always been a puzzle. Four surnames amongst eight brothers and sisters tend to create confusion.

Max's full name was Maxwell Arapata Nene. He was the only one with that surname. He was thirty-five when he died.

'Good luck,' I say to Pete, as I'm leaving.

He grins. That's when I know it's all right. I can come again with my questions. I lean down and kiss Pete on the cheek. He reaches up two fat arms and hugs me tight. We must look rather odd, me half standing, Pete sitting, Max's grave still fresh-earthed beside us. 'Let me know if you find any answers,' I say.

'Hey!' he beams back at me. 'You too 'n all.'

Forty minutes later I'm back in my flat in Mt Albert. I live alone, a situation I have not chosen, and don't pretend to like. Never in all my dreams of return did I imagine a life like the one I'm currently living. But then I never imagined Max either.

To say that Max and I were friends is to imply something

that doesn't hold up when compared with other, ostensibly similar relationships. We *were* friends, but what passed between us had a character of its own; something not duplicated anywhere else in my life. I think I can safely say we challenged each other — that the view of the world each of us had prior to our meeting was altered by the experiences we shared. What I don't know is how Max felt about our friendship. His death has turned everything I believed I knew about him on its head.

One thing I can say with confidence though — Max was as fascinated with language as I am. Early on in our relationship we discovered a shared loathing of jargon. The words associated with the current dogmas, whether social, racial, economic or therapeutic, invariably incited our contempt. It was all to do with freedom. For Max the idea of freedom grew out of a frequently painful physical reality. For me the concept was more metaphysical. Like most practitioners of my craft, I believe language can persuade human beings to almost anything. Take the word 'choice', in Max's view one of the most overused and offensive of words. 'Choices!' he squawked, during our initial encounter, in Paremoremo Prison. (Max, when excited, could sound rather countertenor-ish.) 'Well, I suppose I do have one choice,' he said, bringing his voice back to its normal level ('normal' being a voice so soft I sometimes had difficulty hearing him). 'I can *choose* whether or not to set fire to my mattress.'

It was the kind of joke Max was always making. I laughed that first day, but as I got to know him better my laughter wore a little thin. Max, while in prison, was twice the subject of a suicide watch. Joking about burning his mattress was a sure sign he was close to the edge. Months later, when he began to joke about getting even with a bullying warder, I knew the same edge had been reached. But by then I'd learned to read the signs.

At the beginning, Max and I were simply pupil and teacher. But that relationship quickly became interchangeable. As did the rescuer/rescued juxtaposition. I may have been the rescuer, initially, but that's not how it feels now. My need for Max to explain, to forgive (if that is what's required), is something I struggle with every day. Only Max can move me on from the place I have been stuck in since . . . I was going to say, 'since he died', but of course it goes back further than that, a long way further.

The things that struck me most about Max at our first meeting were his charm, his sense of humour, his ready grin (all the men in Max's family are grinners — it's part of their appeal) and his quirky good looks. It's a testament to his attractiveness that I remember the impression he made on me rather than the environment in which we met. I had never been inside a prison before. Right up to the moment when we shook hands there had been plenty to shock me. But Max's smile, and the boyishness of his manner, disarmed me. The thought that came to me then has stayed with me, in some form, ever since. The man I was looking at was essentially innocent.

I had come to help Max develop his writing skills. The assignment had been entrusted to me by the Society of Authors, of which I was a member. To this day I'm not certain why I took up the challenge. Something to do with a feeling of 'payback', I think. I'd been born into a fortunate home. I'd travelled to England in my early twenties, and stumbled into success as a writer at a time when there was a lot of generosity in the publishing world, and no one talked about the 'market place'. Now that I was back in New Zealand, a happily married woman, I felt indebted. I also, though I didn't know it at the time, needed to get to know my country again. In the fifteen years I'd been away it had become a foreign land.

I had assumed Max's first language would be Maori, but I was wrong. What I came to understand, as our lessons progressed, was that Max had been brought up almost without language. Now that he had time to reflect on his life, he was determined to make up for lost time. He was using me, of course. We both knew that. But at no time did it occur to me that he might be using me for the purposes of revenge. Max never spoke in those terms. What he wanted, what we talked about constantly, was to be at home in both languages. What I didn't understand, and still don't, was whether his wish to master the nuances of English stemmed from his contempt for the Pakeha world, or from a desire, hidden from all of us, to punish.

'Makutu?' Max queried, when I asked him once what he thought about the ancient Maori custom of putting a curse on an enemy. 'Where'd you drag that one up from?'

To say I was intrigued by Max would be to seriously understate the case. I was *fascinated*!

'What do you miss most about your brother?' I asked Pete this afternoon.

His answer came quick and fierce. '*Everything*,' he said.

2

When I took up the Society of Authors' challenge to teach writing to a Paremoremo Prison inmate I had only the vaguest idea of what I was getting into. Gratitude for my good fortune was how I explained to Greg, my husband, and others who shared his doubts, my decision to make the weekly journey to the maximum security prison. At no time did it occur to me to think I might be putting myself in danger.

'You're naive,' my husband complained. 'You have no idea what you're letting yourself in for.'

'I'll be teaching writing skills,' I reminded him. 'What can go wrong with that?'

'You'll see men locked up like animals. You'll be shocked. Appalled. And it *is* shocking. I don't deny it. But those men are there for a reason, and that's what you'll lose sight of, knowing you. I can tell you exactly what will happen, Renate. Every man you speak to will swear to you he's innocent. And you'll believe them. You'll believe every sob story you're told. That's what worries me, how vulnerable you'll be.'

'Vulnerable to what?'

'Manipulation.'

'You could come with me. You're always saying we need to do something about our prisons. You could start by coming to Paremoremo.'

My husband's laugh was not encouraging. 'What as?' he demanded. 'You seem to forget I'm a criminal lawyer. Supporting a limited programme of prison reform doesn't mean . . .'

'You used to be involved. What about that submission you and Dave Wilkinson drew up . . .'

'Dave's lost the plot. Everyone knows that. He'd get rid of prisons altogether, given half a chance.'

'Maybe he's right.'

'When I go to Paremoremo I go to work, Renate, not spend time with some illiterate inmate I don't even represent.'

'The inmate I'm going to see is *Maori*,' I pointed out testily. My emphasis was deliberate. My husband had recently defended a Maori radical on a charge of wilful destruction of property. Citing the legal concept 'colour of right', he argued successfully that his client was innocent on the grounds that he was obeying a higher law than the laws of property. The case, which was widely reported, earned him high praise from the Maori world.

'Maori, Pakeha, it makes no difference,' my husband stated flatly. 'They're all inside for a reason.'

With those warnings echoing in my head I drove into the car park of Paremoremo Prison just before noon on a cool spring Saturday. From the moment I stopped the engine I felt conspicuous. For a start my car seemed to be the only undamaged one on the lot. Then there was the matter of the sticker on my back window. It proclaimed me a member of Greenpeace, whereas all the other stickers I could see advertised Lotto or the local panel beaters. One I passed, on my nervous way to the prison entrance, exhorted me to 'praise Jesus'.

I reached the gates, and looked around at my fellow visitors. Conspicuous again, I thought miserably, glancing down at my jeans. Every other woman was wearing a skirt. Was there a dress code I didn't know about? The few men amongst us were casually dressed in jeans, and sweatshirts or denim jackets. If there *were* rules, they didn't appear to apply to them.

'What brings *you* here then?'

The question was lobbed at me by a warder, a bullish-looking man, with an ugly Belfast accent. I'd been trying to ignore his obvious interest in me. Opening my mouth to answer, I felt myself blush, an appalling tendency of mine. Was I being paranoid, or was everyone eyeing me now? 'I've come to visit Maxwell Nene,' I answered, hoping that would put an end to the scrutiny. 'I'm going to help him with his writing.'

'Well, isn't that somethin' now?'

A ripple of laughter ran through the waiting crowd. Now I was sure of it. Every eye *was* on me. 'He asked for someone,' I explained. 'He wrote to the Society of Authors. That's the . . .'

'So what's Nene going to write about? Raping teenage girls? Drilling policemen fulla lead?'

By this time I felt as if a hundred small fires had been lit inside me. I couldn't believe it was possible to feel so hot on a cool day. 'I imagine he'll want to write about the things he hasn't been able to express till now,' I said, as confidently as I could. 'Everyone knows one of the main causes of violence is . . .'

'Spare us the psychology, sweetheart,' a woman's voice pleaded. 'We get enough of that in there.' She jabbed her elbow, amid laughter, at the prison walls.

Fortunately for me, at that moment the gate in front of us began to open, screeching on its hinges like a medieval drawbridge. As I moved forward thankfully, the warder hissed in my ear, 'If you think this place is fulla frustrated Shakespeares, you're makin' a big mistake. Those are bad men in there, lady. The worst there is.'

To my dismay I found the gate was only the first of three we had to pass through. As it clattered shut behind us we were herded into a wide passageway, where we were obliged to wait till the next barrier was raised. The warder who watched over us at this stage seemed friendlier than his Irish counterpart. He greeted several of the women and children by name. For me, the stranger in the pack, he offered a quizzical smile.

At the third gate we were searched. Emptying the contents of my bag onto the table, the warder, a sour-faced woman with a tongue to match, announced she would be confiscating the dictionary I had brought as a gift for my pupil. 'But Mr Nene asked for it specially,' I protested.

The woman held the book up by its spine, and shook it vigorously. '*Mr* Nene is it?' she scoffed, 'Well whadda you know? He'll get it when we're done,' she added malevolently.

'Do I have your word on that?'

She gave me an incredulous look. Instinctively I leaned back, away from her poisonous smile and stained teeth. 'You're new here, aren't you?' she said. 'You'll learn.'

The final stage of this bizarre journey took me down a long corridor, through a wide door guarded by two men, one Maori, one Pakeha. I would come to know this room well — which corners got the sun, and the best place to position chairs to avoid the constant, eyeballing scrutiny. But that first morning, as I searched the faces milling around me, all I could think was, how do I know which one is Maxwell Nene? In his letter he described himself as a good reader, but a poor writer. The letter was seven pages long. A lot of it didn't make sense. One sentence went on for a page and a half. It began with a reference to the book he was reading, and ended, after many seemingly unrelated parentheses, with a dubious but highly original comment on the Treaty of Waitangi. I was intrigued. Here was a man with so much to say he couldn't stop to organise his thoughts, he just let them pour out. What might he be capable of with the right linguistic tools at his fingertips?

As I waited for my mysterious pupil to reveal himself, I savoured the moment when I would tell the Irish warder that Maxwell Arapata Nene, convicted criminal, had turned out to be New Zealand's answer to Shakespeare.

'Renate Anderson?'

I let out an involuntary gasp, collected myself, and extended my right hand. The man standing before me was smiling so broadly I had the impression his mouth stretched from ear to ear. Perhaps he'd expected an older woman. Or a more bookish-looking one. In any event he seemed pleased to see me.

He led me to the far corner of the room and went in search of chairs. I began to feel like a character in a play — one of those grim Iron Curtain dramas in which individuals struggle to hold on to their humanity in a world ruled by faceless men. I counted eight warders in the room, five leaning against the wall, watching proceedings through hooded eyes, the others quietly prowling. The fact that there were children present, some of whom were busy pushing chairs together to create a makeshift car, all of whom seemed unfazed by the sight of their fathers in prison garb, was a useful corrective to my thoughts. Not everything about this place suggested hopelessness.

As I watched Max make his way towards me, a chair in each hand, I felt a surge of confidence. This man wasn't going to be a problem. My husband was wrong. I'm not sure what I'd expected — an Othello? A warrior from another age? A man who *looked* like a criminal? But Max was none of these things. The only disturbing thing about him, physically, was his tattoos. His face, apart from two small spirals on his cheeks (done in prison, as I learned much later), was unmarked, but his hands looked as if they belonged to a species of blue-striped zebra.

'I'm sorry about the dictionary,' I said, once we'd dispensed with the preliminaries. 'The warder who took it promised . . .'

'Don't worry about it,' Max grinned.

'You'll let me know if you don't get it, won't you? She has no right . . .'

The persistence of his grin stopped me. I'd get used to this habit of his. It would even begin to annoy me. But that first day I saw it as enchanting. That anyone locked up in prison could look so cheerful struck me as something of a miracle.

'Before we start, I should tell you what I'm in for,' Max said.

I shook not just my head but my hands as well. I wasn't ready for a confession. Besides, wasn't he supposed to say he hadn't done whatever it was? 'Another time,' I muttered. 'Let's get to know each other first.'

'Suit yourself,' he answered.

'You *can* tell me one thing though. Whatever you're in for, and I don't want to know, please, I mean it. But . . . did you do it?' I was surprised at myself. I'm not usually so forthright. But I was gambling on being able to tell my husband, when I got home, that he was wrong. I was still a happily married woman then. I wasn't trying to prove a point. All I wanted was a chance to reawaken my husband's passion for social justice, the quality that had first drawn me to him. It distressed me to think of him, a man who'd fought against apartheid, and still, to this day, protested the Labour Party's betrayal of socialism, walking amongst the inmates of Paremoremo, dismissing them as irredeemable.

Max's answer to my question was a verbal *tour de force*. Yeah, he was guilty, but he also wasn't, there were circumstances, things to do with gang life, things I wouldn't understand, about being at a rage and proving yourself and taking the rap and such, but since I didn't want him to tell me what he was in for then he couldn't really explain. But yeah, he was guilty, he deserved to be where he was, and he was sorry, he wished he could remember what happened, he'd tried, but there was nothing, just a blank. Not that he couldn't imagine, he knew what went on, it was the kind of thing you talked about in this place, so he didn't need to remember to know he was guilty. And he wasn't making any excuses. Back then the gang wasn't just on his back, it was in his blood. It was his family, had been for more than half his life, and he wasn't going to go against his family. The night he was busted it was a family thing that was going on, a family thing that went wrong. Of course they were all out of it on booze and dope, but that wasn't an excuse, it was just how things were. And he was going to go on trying to remember because that was important, he'd read books on the subject, and they all said the same thing, that until you remember you don't believe. And until you believe, confront what you did, you can't be forgiven. *I* wouldn't understand of course. How could I? You had to be there to understand, and *there* was another fuckin' planet . . .

As he talked I observed the restless movements of his hands, and the way his eyes kept darting round the room. I observed, too, the curious seesawing quality of his voice. Inevitably, given what I was hearing, I was forced to revise my opinion. Maxwell Nene *was* going to be a problem.

'Sorry about the swearin',' he muttered.

'That's all right.'

'Reckon we could do with a coffee, eh?'

'Is that possible?'

'Sure.' He grinned. '*You'll* have to pay though.'

I followed him through a maze of chairs and children to the other end of the room. Approaching the table from where the coffee was served, I saw a warder pounce on an inmate, who was sitting in the corner with his chair pushed up close to his female visitor. The woman — a wife or girlfriend, I assumed — had spread her skirts over the inmate's lap. The warder wrenched the inmate's chair back, tipping him onto the floor. Max saw where I was looking, and gave me a lopsided smile. It would be another two visits before I understood the meaning of that smile, and worked out for myself why women, whose normal dress was jeans and T-shirts, came to prison wearing long, full skirts.

Serving the coffee was a woman who could have been my mother. I didn't know whether to feel grateful or cross. Like her I was white and middle class. But *I* wasn't here out of charity. I was here because . . .

'D'you mind if I have some biscuits?' Max asked. 'They're five cents each.'

'Have as many as you want.'

When we were seated again I asked Max about the prison library. 'It's shit,' he said. 'Excuse the language, but it is, it's shit.'

I made a mental note to do something about that. It had been obvious to me from the moment I stepped into this room that the majority of inmates were Polynesian. If my husband was serious about the need for prison reform, it shouldn't be too hard to interest him in the library. He was a wealthy man. He could make a difference. More importantly, as a recently appointed QC, he could make people aware. Most New Zealanders simply don't know, I thought, as I scrutinised my surroundings again. These men aren't bad, not irredeemably bad. Look! I silently admonished my fellow citizens. They play with their children; they caress their wives; they laugh, they cry . . .

'So, Max, where shall we start?'

3

I met my husband in London in the autumn of 1990. He'd come over to act in a case that was to go before the Privy Council. We were both guests at a function at New Zealand House to celebrate local artists. I had been on my own for five years. Greg was recently separated from his third wife. By the end of that week it was clear to us both our meeting was predestined. Anyone could see Greg was at a loss without a woman in his life. And I, well, I was at a loss for all sorts of reasons, one of which was my ambivalence towards the country I had abandoned almost fifteen years ago.

Greg was miserable in London. He hated the weather; hated the slights, largely imaginary, which he detected in the accents of his English colleagues; hated the crowds, and the dirt, and Mrs Thatcher's voice on the news every night. About the only thing he liked was the pubs.

'Don't I know you?' were the first words he said to me.

I remember thinking what a nice voice he had, quiet but authoritative. And then I noticed his eyes. They were azure blue, the startling colour you sometimes see in newborn babies.

'You're the author, right?'

I laughed. 'I'm not the only one here tonight,' I said. 'But yes, I am a writer.'

'Renate Anderson.'

'You're not going to tell me you've read my books?'

'Not if I'm under oath. Tell you the truth, I don't read much fiction.'

That was when his face started to make sense to me. I'd seen his photo — a cutting my mother sent me during the Springbok tour. He was one of the organisers of the protest movement. He got himself arrested twice. The only thing I couldn't salvage from the wastepaper bin of my memory was his name.

When, in the next few seconds I learned who he was, several more things fell into place. He was the kind of lawyer journalists liked; partly because his cases tended to be high profile, but also because of his defiant mixing of work and politics. It didn't take me long to fit him into what I knew of other protest movements in New Zealand, in particular the protest against French nuclear testing in the Pacific. By that time his obvious passion for the country I had been planning to return to, on and off, for nearly ten years, had turned me into something of a captive audience. I couldn't get enough of his stories. And I couldn't get enough of his eyes.

'What do you say we absent ourselves? Go find a pub.'

If he hadn't suggested it I would probably have done so myself. For the first time in five years I was aware of grieving, not for one particular person, but for love itself. The wasted years since love had gone out of my life snapped at my heels, driving me into the damp night air; silencing my protest when Greg took my hand and held it tight; suspending disbelief when he declared, before the evening was over, that he had fallen in love with me.

We met again the next day, and the day after that. Greg's case was going well. I shared his relief, and the satisfaction he felt at bettering his opponents. And by the end of the week I had agreed to share his bed. 'I love you,' he kept saying. 'I adore you.'

It seemed incredible to me that a man I barely knew would use such words.

4

The day after my visit to Max's grave I sit down at my desk, determined to clear the messages on my answerphone, and make some inroads into the pile of correspondence that has built up during my absence. Max died nine days ago. The police held on to his body for three days, delaying the tangi which ended, the day before yesterday, with his burial. This morning is the first time I've thought about work in over a week.

I am immediately distracted. Max's face, tucked in amongst a photomontage of friends and family, jumps out at me, destroying all my good intentions. Max presented me with this photo soon after his release. He told me one of his brothers had taken it, but the stamp on the back gave it away as a studio portrait. Max was not conventionally handsome, but in this particular photo he has the smouldering good looks of a modern sex symbol. His hair was still long then, tied back for the occasion in a ponytail. I'm glad he didn't wait till he'd had his hair cut to have the photo taken. Max with his locks shorn was a much fiercer-looking character than the young man I'd got to know in prison. It was as if the anger, which I now accept was never far below the surface, had been etched overnight onto his face, flaring the nostrils wide, staining his broad flat cheeks with the evidence of his crimes. Had he looked that way when I first saw him, I might have formed an altogether different impression.

'Why did you do it?' I remember asking him. 'It suited you long.'

He grinned. He enjoyed wrong-footing me. He especially

liked it when I couldn't explain myself. As if he knew without being told that my objections to his hair, or his clothes, or the company he was keeping, were the inevitable responses of a white, middle-class, do-gooder woman in her mid forties. 'I'm a *gardener*,' he reminded me, emphasising the word to bring home to me that the job was not his choice. (I'd organised the position for him two weeks after his release. At the time I regarded it as an answer to a prayer.) 'You sweat when you garden. Now if I was doing my carving, or writing that novel we talked about . . .'

Max stayed in the gardening job four months. I never did find out what went wrong. His story was that he was no longer needed. 'You're looking at a redundant gardener,' he reported happily. I was angry with him for being so cheerful. He didn't seem to have any idea how hard it was going to be to find another job. When, within days of that conversation, my own life fell apart, Max had the nerve to describe his unemployed status as 'God's opportunity'. 'You want me to deal some shit to that husband of yours?' he offered. 'Because I will, Renate. I'll do whatever you want.'

'What I want,' I told him crossly, 'is for you to find a job.'

His answer was a grin the size of a saucer. 'Jobs aren't the problem.'

But jobs *were* the problem. Increasingly, as the months went by. When I learned from Pete that Max hadn't been made redundant, he'd been sacked, I felt, for the first time, personally betrayed by him. Max, though, had an answer ready. Flashing that grin of his he assured me his sacking had nothing to do with his work, it was his 'tats' the boss didn't like. 'I'd started wearing shorts, see,' he explained. 'One look at my legs, and the poor bastard freaked.'

I take the photo off the wall, and turn it over in my hand. *He nui pohue toro ra raro* I read. *For Renate, from Max. September 1, 1996.* My mood is far from cheerful, but I can't help smiling. Each time I asked Max to translate what he'd written he'd tell me something different. Finally I asked Ani, the eldest of his sisters. Ani lectures in Maori at Manukau Polytech. 'What it means, literally,' she told me, 'is *The convolvulus roots are many and spread below*. But the actual meaning is metaphorical. Something like, *The thoughts of a man's mind are many and secret*.'

'Perfect,' I responded, laughing. 'Max to a T.'

'You should never have cut your hair,' I say out loud to the photo. 'It changed you.'

'Oh yeah?' Max's mocking voice needs little imagining. 'You just liked me better when I was banged up, that's all. Got nothing to do with my hair.'

It's true, I acknowledge. I used to feel so hopeful after those visits to the prison. Max was reading, learning, planning. He even became a Christian. After his release, all I did was worry.

'You thought about that?' his voice challenges. 'You thought how that affected me? Knowing you didn't think I was gunna make it . . .'

'But I never thought that,' I protest out loud. 'I mean, I worry about a lot of people. I used to worry about Greg all the time. That's how I am with the people I love.'

'Didn't do you and Greg much good, did it?'

I slam the photo down on the desk. What right does he have to accuse me? But of course, I concede, I allowed him that right, I made a point of allowing it, as he, always anxious to be fair, permitted me the same licence. The only trouble is, I think now, I never asked the right questions. 'Well, I'm asking them now,' I mutter, as I fit his photo back into the montage. 'We all are.'

And tonight, I remind myself, I'll be asking them of Ani. It was talking to Pete gave me the idea. Ani and Max were close. Or so Max always implied. Ani *must* know something.

I decide to leave the phone messages for later. The thought that there could be one from Max paralyses me. Ten days ago he asked if he could borrow my car to drive down to the King Country. There was to be an unveiling for his Great-Auntie Petula, who died a year ago. I'd told him I'd have to think about it. Last time I lent him the car he was two days late returning it. *And* he'd incurred a speed camera fine.

If he *has* left a message it won't be one I want to hear. Max, when things were going well in his life, was a good-natured man, always willing to help a friend, generous with what little he had. But lately that good-naturedness had been wearing thin. That he was angry about the car was obvious from his reaction when I told him I needed to think about it. Normally he would have laughed, or sent me up affectionately. This time there was silence on the end of the phone. Makutu, I think now. A thing of the past, Max had insisted, but when I heard he was dead it was the word that came into my mind. *A secret curse put on another person to punish him*, is the dictionary explanation. Was Max punishing me when he stole that car and used it, not to go to the King Country, but to commit a crime? It's a question I have to find an answer for.

I've barely made a start on the letters when the phone rings. I consider ignoring it, but realise if I do it will only add to the backlog of unanswered messages. Since the break-up of my marriage I've had to take up a new profession — contract editing. This means I'm dependent on the phone. Actually I have Max to thank that I'm even halfway proficient with the technology of my new job. For a man who spent half his life in institutions he handled everything from computers to lawn mowers with consummate skill. As I pick up the phone I realise he never got round to teaching me how to program the video. That was to be our next undertaking. Will I ever stop missing you? I ask his photo angrily.

'Renate? Maggie Anderson speaking.'

My mouth opens, but no sound comes out. A rogue fist punches my heart. Maggie is Greg's new wife. His fifth. 'You know what he is, don't you?' Max said to me three weeks ago, when the news of Greg's marriage broke. 'He's a serial husband. This one won't last either.'

'Greg's had an accident,' the voice at the other end of the line informs me. I still haven't uttered a sound. 'I thought you should know.'

'Why?'

'Why what?'

Why tell me? is what I want to say. But I can't take in that word, *accident*. Not again. Not after . . .

'Come over! Quick! Come now!' Max's mother Queenie screamed down the phone. 'It's Max. There's been an accident.'

'There's been an accident,' the quiet English voice informed me. A bright, hopeful April day. 'Please, Renate, try and stay calm.'

'I read about Max,' Maggie says. 'I'm sorry.'

'Bet Greg wasn't,' I mutter darkly.

'That's not true.'

'Oh yeah?'

'Look, if you're going to be hostile . . .'

'What sort of accident? Is he badly hurt?'

'He fell asleep at the wheel. He's in Green Lane Hospital . . .' To my surprise and dismay, Maggie's voice breaks. It doesn't fit the pattern. Maggie's not supposed to love Greg. She's supposed to be using him. I'm the one who loves him. As *he* loved *me*, till she came along and spoiled things.

'What's the matter with him?' I ask.

'Broken bones. Dislocated shoulder. Some internal . . .'

'When did this happen?'

'Last night. I'm ringing from the hospital.' Again that break in the voice. It makes me angry. What are a few broken bones beside a young man dead at thirty-five?

'His face is pretty smashed about.'

I think of Greg's face, with its map of lines, and those piercing azure-blue eyes. I think of his voice, the first thing I noticed about him, and his laugh, the way it bubbles up from his stomach. I think of his back with the line of dark hair down the spine, and his chest, which has no hair on it at all. I think of his arms around mine, his hands on my body, his tongue eager in my mouth. In the brief pause before Maggie speaks again I conjure him up so successfully, I can smell the nicotine on his breath.

'He hasn't regained consciousness,' Maggie tells me next. 'They're doing tests now.'

'I'm sorry,' I say. 'It must be . . .'

'Would you come and see him? I need someone to . . . I didn't know who else to call.'

'What about his children?'

'They'll come if . . . Perhaps you didn't know, but Alan's moved out of Auckland. He got a job in Sydney.'

'Cressida? Is she still . . .'

'Living in London? Yes.'

'Poor Greg.'

'And Tim's in Wellington.'

I try to remember what this day was supposed to be about. Catching up on work. Meeting up with Ani. It was never meant to be about Greg. 'What ward is he in?'

'Intensive care . . . When can you come?'

I push the pile of letters to the back of the desk. 'Now, I suppose,' I answer.

'Thank you.'

'I'll see you there then.'

'I hope you don't think . . . I mean, my calling you, I hope you don't think it was inappropriate . . .'

The sound I make starts out as a laugh. 'Appropriate' was another word Max and I outlawed. It was almost as unpopular, in our lexicon, as 'choice'. 'I'll be there in half an hour,' I tell Greg's wife.

5

The only time I know something is true is at the moment I discover it in the act of writing. Those words, from the French novelist Jean Malaquais, so affected me when I first read them, I've almost come to believe I wrote them myself. Writing is about the search for truth. But is it? For most of the latter part of the twentieth century writers have had to live with the notion, propagated by critics and academics, that there is no truth, there are only versions, as numerous as the tellers of tales, of events. When, in the wake of a death from which I know now I will never recover, I wrote *The Cornish View*, whose truth was I endeavouring to serve? The man at the centre of my story, whose alter ego in real life was my friend and lover, was that rare phenomenon, a truly good person. I called him Sebastian. Was it his truth I was celebrating? Or were there darker forces at work? The novel was published, to respectable reviews, at the end of 1986. It seems the things I got right were the things I hadn't had to labour over: the descriptions of Cornwall; the scenes of London life; the sense of two people hopelessly adrift in their personal lives. What I failed to capture was the very thing I'd set out to write about — the uniqueness of the relationship. Most critics found Sebastian and Donna (the woman who could be said to be me, but isn't) tedious. 'Self-obsessed', was a phrase that stuck. 'Awash with a discredited romanticism' was another. Apparently my novel was not about two people in love, as I had thought, but about the impossibility of love in that time of social upheaval (the story covers the years from the late seventies to the mid eighties), something I hadn't set out to write about at all.

So where does that leave my conviction — the nearest thing I have to a credo — that writing, if it's to be any good, has to be about truth?

'You want to know what to write about?' I said to Max, on my third visit to Paremoremo Prison. 'Write about your childhood. That's where most people start.'

I could have told him it wasn't where *I* started, but I wasn't there to talk about myself. Besides, I was curious to know more about this man whose trust I was still trying to win. So far I only had his seven-page letter to go on, but my instincts told me I was dealing with a writer — a potential writer — who would approach words with a child's sense of wonder, sensing their power to capture that elusive thing called truth.

On that particular Saturday Max and I had managed to find ourselves a corner in the small yard that adjoined the visiting room. Never before had I been so aware of the sky. It blazed above us, blue as a field of cornflowers, drawing our eyes upwards, away from concrete walls and wooden chairs and lounging warders. The warmth dribbling on to our hands and faces from the spring sun made me feel light-headed. I found myself wanting the morning to be over so that I could take Greg to bed.

'Childhood sucks,' Max answered.

'Maybe. But that's no reason to . . .'

'Why write about somethin' I wanna forget?'

'Tell me about your family.'

'Nothin' to tell.'

I gestured my exasperation. Had I known then that Max had been put on a suicide watch the day before, I might have handled things differently. But Max, whose trust I believed I was beginning to win — falsely as it turned out — was not in a confiding mood. 'I'm simply following up on what you told me last week, ' I said. 'That you wanted to write something, you felt ready. So . . .'

'I've got a new neighbour,' Max interjected, the words coming out in that strange falsetto voice he used when upset. 'He was bussed in last night. Businessman type. Pakeha. He shouldn't be with us. He shouldn't be anywhere near us jokers.'

'Is that what's upset you?'

'We have a word for eggs like him.'

'Which is?'

'Not fit for a lady's ears.'

I let the remark pass. With Max it wasn't always easy to tell whether he was being serious or not.

'He's a — what's the word? Paedophile.'

'Oh . . .'

'You know what that is?'

'Yes, Max. I know what a paedophile is.'

'Usually they're kept separate. For their own safety.'

'And you think this man is in danger, is that it?'

'I'd stake my life on it.'

'Have you talked to anyone else about this?'

'Give us a break!'

'One of the warders. They're not all bad. You said yourself . . .'

'He's a marked man, Renate. The screws know that as well as I do.'

'Are you suggesting . . .' I shook my head in disbelief. 'Are you saying this man, this paedophile, was put in your block deliberately? That the warders are going to turn a blind eye while he's beaten up, or killed, or whatever. Is that what you're saying?'

'Wouldn't be the first time.'

'That's monstrous.'

'Whaddya expect? This *place* is monstrous.'

'Yes but . . .'

'Look, forget it, eh? Forget I mentioned it.'

'But it's horrible. We have to do something . . .'

Max's laugh set my teeth on edge. 'We?' he parroted.

'Don't pretend you're happy about it.'

He shrugged.

'We have to tell someone.'

'Won't make no difference.'

'It might if I . . .' I hesitated. Greg's voice was in my head,

31

mocking my attempts to understand. 'Rumours, Renate. Rumours and threats. Prisons are full of them. If the authorities stopped to listen to every little whisper . . .'

I looked up at the blue dome above my head. Why were there no birds, I wondered? Then I realised. Birds need trees, and there are no trees around Paremoremo. No bush either. Men can hide amongst trees. They can conceal themselves in bush.

I glanced furtively into the visiting room. None of the men I could see matched Max's description. But then, if you're a paedophile, would you have visitors? I was out of my depth, just as Greg had predicted. I've never met a paedophile. I'm told they're just like other people, they have absolutely no distinguishing characteristics. But how can that be? I don't have children of my own but I knew, even as I struggled to come to terms with what Max had told me, that I would have killed anyone who'd harmed Greg's children in that way.

I stood up. Max, whose expression I couldn't interpret, followed my example. 'You OK?' he asked.

'Let's get coffee.'

'The man's a shithead, Renate. He deserves what's comin' to him.'

Those were our last words on the subject. When I got home I made the mistake of confiding in Greg. The things I'd imagined him saying were uncannily close to what he did say, at greater length, over what should have been a lyrical afternoon.

In the days that followed I found myself scanning the papers for news of an attack at Paremoremo Prison. But if anything was published I never saw it.

I didn't see Max again for three weeks. Greg and I decided to take a holiday. Things had become rather strained between us. The holiday was Greg's idea, but I went along with it happily enough. By the time I saw Max again he'd decided he *was* interested in his childhood after all, one part of it in particular. 'It was that thing you said about kids,' he explained, 'about them being able, you know, to see, not judge and that. About them being uncorrupted.'

'Which isn't the same as being innocent,' I reminded him.

'No. I mean yeah, I agree. Kids can do shitty things, to survive an' that, but it isn't the same as if an adult . . .'

'What are you trying to tell me Max?'

'I've got somethin' for you.' He looked round the room, plunged his hand into the pocket of his jeans, and took out a wad of minutely folded paper. 'Don't wave it about,' he urged, flicking his eyes at the nearest warder. 'We're not s'posed to . . .'

Only when I got home did I realise how much I'd come to accept as normal the strange rituals of prison life. Two months ago I would have protested Max's subterfuge. I would have gone straight to a warder and challenged him to stop me taking the manuscript out of the prison. I was there to teach writing skills. I had every right to take my pupil's work home.

The moment I had the house to myself I started reading Max's story. Later there would be others, with, unlike this first one, almost perfect spelling and punctuation. But there would never be one that moved me more.

The story wasn't long. Written on lined pages torn from a school exercise book, in the untidy handwriting I was already familiar with from his letter, it took only a few minutes to read. But I could sense its power from the start. I was beginning to suspect, from some of the conversations we'd had, that Max was a skilful liar; but this story more than vindicated my belief that when he sat down to write, it was the search for truth that drove him.

Rekon I mustve been 6 or 7. My Mum had just had twins. That made 5 of us kids. I rekon she couldnt cope. Whatever.

I dont remember how I got there. Id have remembered if it was by train. All I remember is my Nan standing at the door with her arms stretched out like those signals you see on old train sets. Big orange arms signaling it was OK I wasnt in trouble any more. Everything was OK.

So. Youre Queenies boy she said.

Her voice was one of the best parts of her after her orange

arms and the way she nearly always smelt of bread. She talked like she was singing. Makes me laugh now when I think about it. People rekon Maori talk that way. You know like we want to burst into song all the time or start dancing. Whatever. Well my Nan wasnt Maori. She was English. From Devon. The only other person I know who talks like my Nan is Renate and shes not Maori either.

The place where Nan lived is called Ohura. Its about halfway between Auckland and Wellington. But its nowhere really. I mean there isnt even a McDonalds. So there I was with my two plastic bags and a skowl plastered across my face wondering what to do about those huge orange arms.

Dont remember how I got inside. Rekon Nan must have given me a shove. She could be pretty fizical Nan. Pushing shoving wacking. Hugging and kissing too though that took longer to get used to. The wacking was normal. What I remember is standing in a room with brown walls like the inside of teapot and the largest tv Id ever laid eyes on blazing away in the corner. Then this voice came out of the back of a chair. Whos this then?

Jesus I thought. A house with talking chairs!

Come and say hullo to your grandfather Max.

Dunnow what I expected to see. A man shaped like a chair? A monster with two heads? Dr Spock?

Cat got your tongue the chair monster growled.

In the days that followed I would lern a lot about that chair. My grandfather hardly ever left it for one thing. Only to go to the dunny or down the road to by more beer. When either of those things happened and if Nan wasnt looking Id go and sit in the chair and pretend I was Ganda (thats what I called him) and drink beer out of the bottle hed have left on the floor as if he just knew I was going to finish it off for him. Id been drinking beer ever since I could remember so it didnt make me sick or anything. Well one time it did but I was sick then anyway.

Usually I heard Ganda coming back and made myself scarce with plenty of time to spare. The few times I didnt move fast enuf I got a belting. They werent too bad. Nuthin like the beltings Id been getting from Mums boy friend Sam (Sam the Sadist I call him now but I was just a dumb little kid then and didnt have words).

Gandas real name was Tom. He was Maori. But he could have been from Siberia for all the difference it made. He had a sister called Great Auntie Petula who was a real Maori but he didnt seem to like her very much. The few times she came to visit all they seemed to do was snap at each other.

This is Queenies eldest Nan explained to the chair monster. Hes come to live with us.

The spilled light from the television hit my grandfathers eyes as he turned his head to look at me. White eyes with blood in them. Definitly a monster. I tried to see if his ears curled like Dr Spocks but apart from the fact that they sprouted frizzy black hairs I couldnt see anything pekular.

Come here for some decent tucker have you boy? That daughter of mine forget to feed you?

I could see his hand moving down the sides of the chair. I think I guessed then that that was where he kept his money. The money Nan didnt know about. I was used to people hiding their money. My mum did it all the time.

Dont you mind your grandfather lad Nan said. His bark is worse than his bite.

Whod be scared of that old reck I thought as I followed Nan through to the kitchen. I could knock him over with one hand.

Your stomak must be thinking your throats been cut Nan said as she ladeled rabbit stew and potatos on to my plate.

Nans rabbit stew was the greatest. Like her bread and the trifel she made with stale sponge cake. When people ask me what happines is I say its sitting at my Nans kitchen table watching her ladel food on to a plate. Happines is when the thing youve been hoping for comes true. Its hope with the outcome already tipped in your favour. Thats what happines is.

The way to a mans heart is through his stomak Nan said as I tucked into the spuds and stew. And your my wee man now Max arent you?

❋

35

'Ani? It's Renate. Listen, I'm sorry, but I'm not going to be able to make it tonight. Can we change it to tomorrow?'

'Where are you calling from? Sounds like you're at sea.'

'I'm at Green Lane Hospital.'

Ani's sharp intake of breath is followed by two quick-fire questions, 'What's happened? Are you all right?'

'It's Greg. My husband. *Ex*-husband. He's been in a car accident.'

'I didn't know you still saw him.'

'I don't.'

'Then why . . .'

'Damn! My card's running out. I'll explain when I see you. Tomorrow same time?'

Ani's answer is lost in the beeping of the telephone. I curse under my breath. That Ani knows more than she's letting on about Max's death has grown in my mind from a suspicion to a conviction. She knows more about his life too. I'm certain of that. But Ani, known in the family as 'the ghost' because of her habitual elusiveness, is not an easy person to pin down. That she agreed to see me at all, so soon after the tangi, is something of a miracle.

I turn from the phone booth, and walk across the shiny hospital foyer, with its oppressive smell of flowers, to where Greg's wife is waiting for me. It occurs to me she might have spent the night here. If she has, it doesn't show. Expensive jeans; pale gold jacket; that chunky jewellery you see everywhere these days; carefully applied make-up. There's nothing casual about this woman's appearance.

Our eyes meet. Somewhere between seeing her at the entrance to the hospital, ducking out of sight so I could make my call to Ani, and now, mere minutes later, my bitterness towards her, nursed over the two years she has lived with Greg, has evaporated. I touch the sleeve of her jacket. 'Let's go,' I say.

6

I was a different person when I lived with Greg. It pains me to say it, but I felt whole then; able to tackle whatever challenges came my way. Most probably I would never have got involved with Max had I been living on my own. It isn't a question of confidence — although mine has taken a heavy battering in the last two years — it's more to do with energy; energy and hope. I was full of hope when I lived with Greg: hope for our marriage; hope for my work; hope for the country I'd returned to after an absence of fifteen years. It's not that I would describe myself as hope-less now, just subdued. Not once in the almost seven years I was with Greg did it occur to me that the marriage could end. The day it did I plunged into a state of shock deeper even than the shock I felt on being told Max was dead. Nothing hitherto had prepared me for either event. Greg and I had our differences, Max being one of them, but that he would declare the marriage over, without explanation, was unthinkable. As unthinkable as Max's death.

'If they let him out, he's not coming here. No way,' Greg said, when I told him Max's parole hearing was due.

'Well of course he isn't,' I protested. 'Whatever made you think . . .'

'You've been going to see him for the best part of two years. I know you, Renate. You can't tell me you're not in love with him.'

'That's nonsense.'

'Is it? Why don't you try asking your friends? The ones you

37

used to see so much of before this savage came into your life.'

I remember the difficulty I had staying calm. We'd had many exchanges of this kind. I knew how nasty they could get. But I clung to the hope that if Greg could just meet Max, if he'd take the time to talk to him, to read the stories he was writing, to see for himself the exquisite bone carvings he was producing, everything would change. 'Savage' was unworthy of Greg. He's not a racist. As a lawyer his defence of Maori has been every bit as vigorous as his defence of Pakeha. No, I told myself, Greg's anger isn't with Max, it's with me.

'Do you know what I think, Renate? I think those years you spent out of New Zealand clouded your judgement. This isn't some war orphan you're dealing with, some innocent victim of circumstances. This is a man who's raped and killed. They don't come much more evil than that.'

It wasn't the first time Greg had thrown those words at me, but it was the first time I'd stayed silent in the face of his attack. I'd known for over a year what Max was in prison for. I'd tried not to know, but I kept stumbling over the information despite all my attempts to avoid it. I won't say it made no difference to our relationship. It made a great deal of difference. But after months of anguish I'd managed to store the information in a safe place in my head — a place I tried hard never to visit. Maybe Greg guessed that was my way of coping. Maybe that's why he liked to remind me, as often as he could, of exactly what I was dealing with.

I look down at the man who was my husband and feel nothing. His head is propped up on several pillows, but when I try to focus on his face my vision blurs. His hands, lying on top of the sheet, look as if they need a wash. As does his hair, spread like unravelled wool across the pillow. He has a tube coming out of his mouth, another out of his neck, a third attached to a wrist, a fourth that disappears under the bedclothes.

'What are they all for?' I ask Maggie, pointing to the tubes.

'Search me,' she answers. 'The doctor did explain, but . . .'

I look again at Greg's face. This time my eyes behave themselves. What I see are two lines of ugly stitches marching across his cheeks. It's not too bad, I decide. Those stitches will go. And if there are scars they'll give him a piratical look . . . Then I see that his jaw is in a different place from where it used to be. It's as if he's been savagely kicked. His whole face is out of alignment.

Now it's Maggie I can't bring myself to look at. Maggie was a model once. I've never thought about it before but I suppose if you've lived that life you never really stop thinking about your appearance. You must be hating this, I think. You must be wishing you were anywhere but here. 'The children,' I say, 'are they . . .'

'Tim's on his way,' Maggie answers. 'Alan will come if . . . if I think . . .'

'I'm sure it won't come to that.'

'I haven't been able to contact Cressida. She's on holiday in Greece.'

'She was always the favourite,' I remark pointlessly.

On impulse I take Greg's hand. I hear Maggie's sharp intake of breath. Greg's hand is warm, but otherwise lifeless. 'You're not to die,' I instruct his inert body. 'You lying here, it's all wrong. They can do wonders now. Bring people back from the dead. You're not to die!'

I glance at Maggie. I expect to see disapproval written on her face, but what I read is a plea for help. 'Don't worry about *him*,' is what I sense her signalling. 'Help *me*!'

It was the need for help that brought Maggie into our lives. Specifically, her need of Greg's legal expertise; but also, as I realised too late, Greg's need to overcome his chronic fear of abandonment. 'You shouldn't leave him alone so much,' Maggie said to me, in what I thought was a joke, but see now was a warning. 'He may be a tiger in court, but he's a pussycat at home. Isn't he?'

I was astounded at the intimacy both of her words, and the smile she bestowed on me as she uttered them. We'd only just met. Greg, having taken her on as a client, had invited her to dinner; in itself an unusual enough event to arouse my suspicions. Now here she was, talking while Greg was temporarily out of the room, as if she'd known him all her life.

'You'll like her,' Greg had assured me earlier. 'She's in the most awful trouble, but it doesn't seem to get her down.'

'Remind me what she was arrested for.'

'Home invasion and theft. With destruction of property. Fortunately bail was fixed low, otherwise I might have had to pitch in myself. Her looks helped of course.'

'Naive', Greg called me when I first talked to him about Max. 'Vulnerable to manipulation.' Why didn't I remember those words as I watched my husband that night, following the twists and turns of Maggie's conversation, laughing when she laughed, encouraging her to confess and confide; to treat us both as friends? I remember thinking how handsome he looked, with his ivory cigarette holder balanced in his fingers, and his blue, blue eyes alight with interest. He served our best wine too, something else which should have alerted me. But by the end of the evening I was as much under Maggie's spell as he was.

'I like her,' I remarked, truthfully, as we stood on the verandah waving goodbye. 'She's got guts.'

'Got a good head on her shoulders too,' Greg responded.

'Will you get her off?'

'Sure as hell hope so.'

'I thought there was a rule about not getting involved with your clients.'

Greg gave me a quizzical look. 'That's rich, coming from you,' he said.

'How do you mean?'

'You seem to be getting pretty involved with Maxwell Nene.'

'I'm his teacher. I'm supposed to be involved.'

'And I'm supposed to do everything in my power to get justice for Maggie Leathart.'

That visit was the first of many. By the end of the week it was established that Maggie would join us every Friday night for a family meal. If we were having one of our rare parties — a

Sunday lunch or Saturday dinner — she would be included as a matter of course. 'She's lonely, poor woman,' Greg kept reminding me. 'And though she hides it well, she's scared.'

Then Greg and I went away on holiday and Maggie temporarily slipped out of focus. But it was her case Greg was to deal with on his return. She wouldn't stay out of focus for long.

I have to admit the facts of Maggie's case were extraordinary. At the height of her modelling career she married a television producer, Paul Leathart, whose appetite for the high life had already attracted the attention of the gossip columnists. Their wedding, as reported to me by Greg (I was still living in England at the time), was a huge celebrity affair.

Within months of their marriage Maggie was hired as a presenter of children's television. 'There was a lot of backbiting when it happened,' Greg told me. 'Accusations of nepotism, that kind of thing. But Maggie took it all in her stride. Luckily for her she doesn't have your thin skin.'

What happened then is the plot of a soap opera. First Maggie was fired, on a charge never made public, but rumoured to be the result of a drinking spree, then her husband was arrested on a fraud charge. The timing of these events — the marriage, the high-profile careers, the public disgrace — isn't clear, but I assume we're talking years, not months. Certainly by the time she came into our lives Maggie had been divorced from her husband for a number of years. Paul had served a six-month sentence and Maggie was living alone in, I assumed from what Greg had told me, straitened circumstances.

How she came to choose Greg as her counsel I will never know. She was not on legal aid — she made a point of letting me know that the first time she came to dinner — so I can only speculate as to how she planned to pay Greg, whose fees I would have described, had I been his client, as astronomical.

The charge against her was that on the night of 23 October 1995, she broke into her ex-husband's flat and stole a number of valuable items, amongst which were a pair of gold cuff links, a thirty-year-old bottle of whisky, a Hotere painting, a Victorian travelling clock and a large sum of cash. Most of what remained was systematically trashed, leaving her to face a charge of home invasion. When, subsequently, the entire stash of stolen goods was found in her flat, her defence was that these were her matrimonial property, withheld from her at the time of the divorce because of the police proceedings against her husband. She denied breaking and entering, pointing out that she had her own key. When her husband disclaimed all knowledge of the key, describing his ex-wife as the last person in the world he would allow into his flat, Maggie promptly labelled him a liar. As for the damage to property, that was explained, by Maggie herself and by Greg in court, as an unfortunate consequence of Maggie forgetting to lock the door behind her.

The case was heard before the District Court in Auckland at the beginning of April, 1996. Greg, according to all the reports, was in fine form. Maggie, whose face kept smiling out at me from the television screen, was described in the press as 'the matronly but still magnificent Maggie Leathart'. When she was found not guilty, Greg punched the air with his fist. That night he took Maggie out to dinner. 'Didn't want to put you to the trouble of cooking,' he explained, when he phoned to tell me.

Now Greg lies near death on a hospital bed, and Maggie looks like the loneliest woman in the world.

'If it's any comfort,' I say to her, 'I was told once by a clairvoyant that Greg would live into his nineties.'

She gives me a look I can't interpret.

I let go of Greg's hand. If I was a decent person I'd walk round to Maggie's side of the bed and give her a hug. But the thought turns my body to lead. 'What do you want from me?' I ask. I try to make the question sound casual, but if *I* can hear the resentment in my voice then so can she. I don't love Greg any more. That's what I told Max last time he asked. I don't owe him, or Maggie, anything.

'Do you think . . . that clairvoyant . . . would she see *me*?'

Oh God, I respond silently, why don't I keep my big mouth shut?

'It's not just Greg, whether he'll get better or not, it's . . . oh shit, Renate! Why is everything such shit?'

'Do you want to go for a coffee?'

'We should never have got married. *Big mistake.*'

I open my mouth in astonishment. I'd said those words myself, to my friend Tess, the first time she visited me in my flat. But this marriage is only three weeks old. Surely disillusionment can't have set in already?

'Coffee,' I say sternly.

Maggie leans down, and kisses Greg on the cheek. I catch a glimpse of her large white breasts. Since giving up modelling Maggie has become plump. I think plump's the word, not fat. Though there have been times when I've described her, without apology, as a 'fat old cow'. I've even heard myself criticising her clothes which, if I'm honest, I rather envy. 'Mutton dressed as lamb.' I've trotted that one out a few times. Along with references to dyed hair and make-up put on with a trowel.

The café is bleak, filled with people whose slumped posture suggests a common weariness. I buy Maggie coffee and a doughnut. She ignores the doughnut and takes out a cigarette. 'No smoking!' the woman behind the counter calls out.

'Stuff you!' Maggie yells back.

Suddenly the café is filled with a dangerous energy. The woman behind the counter is Maori. Is Maggie going to take her on? The No Smoking sign is plainly visible on the wall behind the counter.

For a few tense seconds every eye is on Maggie. Then she stubs out her cigarette. Disappointment filters through the air like cigarette smoke. An altercation between two ageing women, one Maori, one Pakeha, would have created a welcome diversion for the weary patrons.

'This country is shit,' Maggie says, as she stuffs her cigarettes back in her bag. 'You should have stayed in England.'

'I'm not sure it's so very different.'

'It's got a Labour Government, hasn't it?'

'So have we.'

43

'Soiled goods, most of them. Look at their records.'

'I didn't know you were political, Maggie.'

She laughs. It's not the kind of laugh you can share, so I stay silent. Can Greg and Maggie have argued about politics, I wonder? I can remember times when Greg argued in favour of the late, unlamented centre-right coalition. So far as I know he's always voted Labour but I'd noticed, in my last year with him, that his attitudes were becoming increasingly right wing. Especially, and painfully for me in view of my friendship with Max, in regard to crime.

'Where was Greg going?' I ask. 'He hates driving at night. Was he going to see a client?'

'We'd had a row,' Maggie answers. 'A real humdinger. Plates smashed, obscenities hurled, the lot.'

'Had he been drinking?'

'Don't you mean, had *I* been drinking?' Maggie's eyes, level with mine, are like shards of polished steel. 'You might as well say it, Renate. It's what everyone thinks.'

'I asked you about Greg.'

'You've lived with him. When does he not drink?'

I nod. I wonder if we're both thinking the same thing — that if I'd been a drinker Greg and I might still be together.

'Of course we'd bloody well been drinking,' Maggie admits. 'I sit in that great house all day long, no neighbours, not ones you'd want to talk to, no car, Greg has to have the car, and anyway I can't be trusted behind the wheel, can I? As for buses, forget it. You wouldn't have known about buses, would you Renate? You had your own car. Well, let me tell you, in this great city of ours, you can wait an hour for a bus. An hour! Told you this country was shit.'

I glance at my watch. If I go back home I'm not going to be able to work. The day has been effectively sabotaged. 'Do you want me to sit with him this afternoon?' I suggest, not, it has to be said, with much show of enthusiasm. 'You could take my car. Go home and have a sleep or something.'

'Why would you want to do that for me?'

I wave the question away with my hand.

'Greg always said you were a pushover.'

'Look . . .'

'Sorry. No, really . . . I can be a prize bitch sometimes. I'm sorry.'

'Do you want the car or not?'

'It was Max. He was jealous of Max.'

'He had no need to be.'

'When has Greg ever needed a reason?'

I drain the last of my coffee, and push my chair back. Already I'm beginning to regret my offer.

Maggie, perhaps sensing my regret, lowers her head. Exhaustion, I assume, or a sudden paroxysm of grief. But it's neither. It's the doughnut, which she begins to shovel into her mouth. I watch, fascinated. How can she cram so much food in and still breathe? Eventually she lifts her head, and swills down the last of her coffee. Then she wipes her mouth on the paper napkin, and says, 'I'm not in Greg's will. That's what we were quarrelling about. He's left everything to his children.'

At the end of my long afternoon at the hospital I call in to see my friend Tess. Like me Tess works at home — she's a biographer, in my view the best in the country. We've known each other so long we can practically read each other's thoughts. Which doesn't mean we always agree about things. I've never doubted Tess' loyalty, or her love, but there have been times when our differences have led to days, even weeks, of estrangement. Today turns out to be one such occasion.

'You're pathological, you know that?' Tess rages at me. 'Have you forgotten what that creep did to you?'

'No worse than what David did to you.'

'David's my daughter's father. There's a difference. And anyway, he didn't lock me out of my own home.'

'Only because he lacked the imagination.'

Tess, whom I would normally describe as 'serene', gives me a look of such anguished frustration it's all I can do not to laugh.

The trouble is, I know she's right. I shouldn't be going to see Greg. I shouldn't be having anything to do with him. Since I came back to New Zealand, Tess has been the only person I've trusted enough to confide in. She understands, better than I do myself, the 'pathology' of my marriage. So why can't I heed her advice? She's known me since I was seven years old. We went through secondary school and university together. We both became writers. It's idiotic for me to set myself against her. Without her I might well have gone under in the terrible days after Greg left.

'Don't suppose you've got any wine in the fridge, have you?' I suggest.

'Renate Anderson, you give a whole new meaning to the word stubborn,' she throws back at me.

7

There's only one word to describe Ani and that's *beautiful*. I suppose the word might have been used to describe Maggie when she was Ani's age, but the difference is Ani's beauty is natural, whereas Maggie's . . . But I don't want to think about Maggie. Or Tess, whose anger, fuelled by anxiety, abated only slightly as we drank our wine. I want to think about Max.

Like Max, Ani had a Maori father, a relative, Max told me once, of his own father. Beyond that I know very little about her. I didn't even know her surname till recently. Max's family stories were always so contradictory it was impossible to distinguish truth from fantasy. One day he'd swear what he was telling me was gospel; the next he'd say he'd made it all up. But Ani's beauty has never been in dispute. Those high cheekbones, that perfect skin, her athlete's body, are there for all to see.

'Can I ask you something?' I say. We're sitting in the living room of Ani's Manurewa flat. It's the day after my visit to the hospital. I've never been here before. I have to admit the place has taken me by surprise. White sofa and chairs, bare white walls, black dining table against the inside wall — it's the apartment of a busy executive, not a Maori language teacher. Though the carving on the coffee table in front of me is Maori.

'You're going to ask me if it's Max's,' Ani guesses, nodding at the enlarged bone fish-hook that has been attracting my attention. Mounted on a carved wooden plinth, it's an impressive piece of work. I even wonder if the minimalism of the rest of the room is deliberate; designed to enhance this stark reminder of how Ani's — and Max's — people once lived.

I smile at her. 'Is it?' I ask.

She nods. 'He made it for me in prison.'

'Actually,' I confess, after a brief but not uncomfortable silence, 'that wasn't what I was going to ask.'

'Oh?'

'Though it was about Max.'

Ani raises an elegant eyebrow.

'Was he always a liar?'

For a moment I think I've blown it. There's no perceptible change in Ani's expression, but I feel the temperature in the room drop several degrees. I brace myself for an attack, but instead what happens is that Ani laughs. I'm so relieved, I laugh back. 'My sister has a great line in dirty jokes,' Max told me once. 'You'd never think it to look at her.'

Will Ani and I ever know each other well enough to exchange jokes? I wonder.

'I'm the wrong person to ask, Renate,' Ani says. 'The one you want is Pete. Or Lily. I know I'm closest to Max in age but . . . well, I guess you know by now what kind of a family we are. If the word *dysfunctional* didn't exist they'd have had to invent it to describe us.' She laughs again, putting me at my ease. Or am I being fobbed off? Reminded in the nicest possible way that Max is the family's business, not mine. 'You know what the whanau call me, don't you?' she goes on. 'The ghost.'

'Only because you don't live with them.'

'Oh, it's more than that, my friend. It's a whole lot more than that.'

'The family . . .' I begin, hesitantly, because I'm not at all sure this line of questioning will get me anywhere. 'Why did they never visit Max in prison?'

'Is that what he told you?'

'Uh huh.'

The smile fades from Ani's eyes. She uncrosses her legs, and turns her head so that she's looking, not at me, but at the window. The curtains — pale green, almost the only colour in the room — are drawn, but the lights from the steady stream of passing cars dance over the surface of the material, so that it seems at any moment those curtains will swing open, exposing us to those relentlessly probing beams.

'You know what Max did, don't you? You know what he was in for?'

The words are spoken quietly, almost without expression. 'Yes,' I reply. 'Though I never wanted to. At some level I felt it didn't really matter.'

'It mattered to our mother,' Ani says.

'So that's why she didn't visit . . .'

Ani turns to look at me. There's not a shred of make-up on her face (again I contrast her briefly, and unkindly, with Maggie), yet in the glow from the reading lamp beside the sofa she looks as if she's been made up by an expert. Her shoulder-length hair is black one moment, burgundy the next. Her eyes are the eyes of a doe caught in the headlights of a car. I asked Max once if being called a ghost — Queenie uses the word all the time — was an insult. Typically he didn't answer my question directly. 'There's a lotta stuff going on in Ani's life,' he said. 'I understand, even if Queenie and them don't.'

'Do you know how far it is from Mum's house to Pare?' Ani asks me now. There's no hint in her voice of the menace I sense in her words. 'Have you thought about how much that costs in petrol? That's providing there's a roadworthy car on hand. And money left over from the dole.'

Several sharp rejoinders occur to me, but I'm too conscious of my burning cheeks to risk opening my mouth. I know where Queenie lives *and* I know how poor she is. I don't need Ani to remind me. Economic restraints — which I'm experiencing myself now I live alone — are something I've been aware of all my adult life. Fifteen years of self-employment in London taught me a lot about inequality. And injustice. The Maori part of Queenie's life may have been a revelation to me, but the poverty needed no explaining.

'More wine?' Ani offers, sliding off the couch, and reaching for the bottle I'd brought with me as koha.

I hold my glass out gratefully. The interrogation would seem to be over.

With our glasses refilled, conversation resumes. It's not Max we talk about now but Ani's work, and mine; the kind of easy exchange of information between single women who are getting to know each other. Twice while we're chatting the phone rings, but Ani ignores it. 'Answerphone,' she explains, when I express concern.

Ani must be thirty-four. That she's never married is extraordinary enough to attract comment. It's not so much that she's beautiful as that, in choosing spinsterhood (I assume she has chosen it), she's going against the culture of both her family and her race. Her two sisters, Ela and Lily, were both married in their teens, Ela because she was pregnant, and Lily because she wanted to be. I know nothing of Ani's personal life. If there have been boyfriends no one's ever mentioned them. All I know is what Max told me, and that didn't amount to much.

'Ani is special,' he said to me, the day he drove me to Manukau College to meet her. 'She has a vision.'

'What kind of a vision?'

'She's a leader, you know? She sees further than other people. She'll be a kuia one day. She already is, in a way.'

Remembering Max's words now I wonder if Ani's reluctance to reveal anything of herself in this flat, or in her conversation with me for that matter, could have a political explanation. Max and I used to talk a lot about the Maori protest movement. How far should it go? What was the true significance of the Treaty? What did Maori mean by sovereignty? But I never heard Max mention Ani in this context, not directly anyway. The person whose name came up most, at least in the beginning, was Greg. I wanted Max to admire Greg for his defence of Maori in court. But of course that was when my marriage, and my optimism, were still intact.

An hour later the bottle of wine is empty. I feel I should leave, but I'm reluctant to walk away knowing no more than when I arrived. I'm grateful that Ani hasn't questioned me about Greg.

I told her he was out of danger when I got here, but I said nothing about the afternoon I'd spent at his bedside. I'd expected those hours to be haunted by memories of my marriage, but the ghost who visited me came from the time before Greg. When Maggie came back, just before six, I was able to tell her what the doctors had told me, that Greg's condition was still considered critical, but he was in no immediate danger. What I didn't tell her was that the nurses thought I was Greg's wife.

'I haven't been very helpful, have I?' Ani surprises me by saying. We've just come to the end of a conversation about the Maori language schools established throughout the country in recent years. I'd questioned the value, in the present economic climate, of having Maori as a first language. I agreed with Ani that Maori must and should be taught, but argued that, as it's not the language of commerce or the internet, it could only ever be a personal or cultural tool. Ani's reaction brought the blood rushing back into my cheeks.

'You talk as if you think Pakeha society is indestructible,' she said. 'You sound just like your colonising forebears. The English language, English institutions, God Save the Queen — no other way of governing is possible.'

I protested, of course. I don't think like that at all. But Ani was not to be stopped. 'You know what your ancestors believed, don't you?' she scoffed. 'That Maori were a dying race. Our demise was regrettable, a sad consequence of Empire, but what could be done? The March of Civilisation must go on.'

Listening to her I thought how close her views were to those of her dead brother. Which made it all the more strange that Max never talked of her in that context. To listen to him you'd have thought Ani was a seer of some kind, a female tohunga, engaged on a spiritual, not a political, odyssey. Or am I just being ignorant, and the two journeys are the same?

'You didn't come here to discuss te reo Maori,' she says now. I grin at her. 'I'm not complaining,' I say.

'Max never lived with Mum, you know. Well, not after the age of six.'

I nod. I already know this, from Max's writing, but I don't want to admit it in case it stops her talking.

'Once the twins were born there wasn't really room for him.'

Again I nod. I'm watching her as closely as I can without being rude. I don't want to miss even the smallest change of expression.

'After Max left, Mum and Sam got married.'

'Sam?' I enquire innocently. This would be the 'Sam' Max mentioned in his writing. 'Sam the Sadist', he called him. He wouldn't tell me why.

'Sam Etuata,' Ani goes on. 'Father of the twins. Vincent was born later.'

'Etuata. That's a Samoan name, isn't it?'

'Yep.'

'What was he like? You must remember him.'

Ani's head flicks to one side, a gesture that reminds me of Max.

'His name came up a few times,' I say, hoping this will encourage her. 'But Max never seemed to want to talk about him.'

Ani's response is an impassive stare. It's a look I've seen before on the faces of Max and his family. I call it their 'opaque' look. Since I can't very well stare back, I turn my attention to Max's carving, and look at that instead. Finally, when it's become obvious Ani has said all she's going to say about Sam Etuata, I ask her what she knows about Max's time in Ohura. I may not be getting answers, but I am getting a clearer sense of where to look for them. Sam Etuata was the only person in the family Max never wanted to talk about. Now Ani is showing a similar reticence. That has to mean something.

'Max was never at Ohura Prison, was he?' Ani says.

'Not the prison. When he was a kid.'

'Oh . . . then. Yeah. I do remember something. Bits and pieces. Mum's parents lived in Ohura. Yeah . . . I remember Mum telling me to say goodbye to Max because he was going away to live with his grandparents. Don't think I ever did though . . . say goodbye.'

'Did you meet them? Your grandparents.'

'That's it. I remember now. My grandmother died while Max was living there.'

'What about your grandfather?'

'He's dead now too.'

'And you never met him either?'

'Nope.'

'Seems odd.'

Ani grins. She has Max's grin, cheeky and challenging at the same time. 'Why?' she asks. 'Because you think all Maori families are close?'

'Didn't you even go to the tangi?' I ask back.

The grin disappears. 'You'd have to ask Mum about that,' Ani says.

Shortly after that our conversation falters. Nevertheless I'm disappointed when Ani makes no attempt to stop me leaving. There's still so much I want to ask. Who was the girl at Max's tangi, for instance, the one who couldn't stop crying? And what was Max's connection with the casino? (Something I only learned about after he died, from Pete.) I'd even planned to ask whether the gang Max once belonged to, and which he swore in prison he'd renounced, might have had something to do with his death. But I'd reckoned without Ani's imperviousness to questions.

As we say our goodbyes, the fact that I have been told almost nothing I didn't know already hits me like a punch in the ribs. How can I hope to solve the mystery when the questions I ask, even the ones I get answers to, plunge me deeper into confusion? After talking with Pete I thought there was a level of agreement between us. The family was part of the mystery of what went wrong for Max, but what we had to concentrate on was his life in prison, and after. Now, with Ani's enigmatic words echoing in my head, I'm not even sure I got it right with Pete. Everyone in Max's family, it seems, has something to hide.

'You think most Maori, most respectable Maori, accept the situation, don't you?' Max said to me, during one of our conversations about sovereignty. 'We're an integrated peoples, isn't that what you believe? But that's all bullshit, Renate. The radicals, they're not the fringe, they're the voice of an otherwise silent majority.'

'I don't believe that,' I protested. 'If it were true, the tribes wouldn't be lodging Treaty claims. They'd be throwing petrol bombs into Parliament.'

For some reason that made Max laugh. 'There's something you don't understand about the Treaty, Renate,' he said. 'It doesn't work the same way for Maori as it does for Pakeha. *You* see it as a way of redressing the wrongs of history. We see it as the latest in a long line of weapons. You have to hand it to us; we're an adaptable race. We adapted to muskets pretty damn quick. Then when warfare didn't get us what we wanted we tried passive resistance. Lately we've had a go at protest marching. Another thing we adapted from you Pakeha.'

'Yes, but . . .'

'From Hone Heke to Whina Cooper and the Waitangi Tribunal is one unbroken line,' Max declared. 'The protests won't stop until sovereignty is restored to us.'

The way he spoke reminded me of the Hyde Park orators I used to listen to on summer Sundays. Only they were usually talking about flying saucers, or the end of the world, not the sovereignty of a colonised people.

Reaching my car, I pause to look up at the sky. The traffic has eased. Only the occasional beam of light dims the brilliance of the stars, and the full-cream glow of the moon.

I glance up at Ani's window. From where I'm standing the curtains look gold, not green. 'Make Greg better,' I say to the God I only half believe in. 'Give him back to Maggie. I don't want any more deaths.'

'So what d'you think you're doing, visiting that old fart in hospital?' Max's voice accuses, as I start up the engine. 'Hasn't he done enough to you?'

'None of your business,' I respond angrily.

'That's the problem with you, Renate, you've got no fuckin' judgement.'

8

It was Nan taught me to read. If I couldve stayed with her if she hadnt died I wouldnt be needing these writing lessons.

Now young man she said that first day we will have none of your lax city ways in this house. Your grandfather can ruin his eyes and adil his brains with television but you and me is gunna read books.

And that was how it was every single day. Ganda in his chair watching tele Nan and me in the kitchen reading books. And they werent kids books neither. Nicholas Nickelby and King Solomon's Mines and a book of yarns by a bloke called Hilaire Belloc. If I yawned or shifted my chair so I could see the tele Nan would wack me across the ear. That hurt Id yell. And shed laugh and say something like not as much as it hurts to be ignorant in this world.

I really loved my Nan. I couldve listened to her voice all day. Even when she was angry. And she was that plenty of times. Like my first day at school when I did a runner. I got that many wacks with the wooden spoon the bloody thing split down the middle. Got called names Id never heard before too. Polecat and Ragamuffin and Dunce. I tried to tell her school was for girls but that only made her worse. In the end I promised I wouldnt do it again and I didnt neither.

Looking back I realize I mustve already been to school in Auckland but I cant remember anything about it. All I remember is the school in Ohura and the teacher Mrs Holland who made us say things in Maori even though her skin was as white as my Nans. When she realised the only Maori I knew was Kia Ora she told me shed soon put that right. Well make a little warrior of you yet Max she said. What do you say to that?

Mrs Holland wore a pinafor over her dress and she smelt of soap. Some days she got chalk marks on her cheeks and Id go up to her and tell her her face was dirty. I did it the first time as a dare but it didnt work cause she didnt get angry. After that every kid in the class wanted to tell her about the chalk.

Things wouldve been different if Id stayed in Ohura.

I put the exercise book down, and let my head drop into my hands. I'm not long back from Ani's. It's late. My desk is a mess. The winking light on my answerphone tells me I have thirteen messages. Max was so still in his coffin. A fly played around his mouth and he never moved. I went to shoo the fly away, but Queenie stopped me. 'We don't do that,' she admonished gently.

Where are you, Max? Where have you gone?

Of all the things Max wrote for me the Ohura story is the one I return to most often. We even discussed using it as the first chapter of a novel. Once he'd mastered the basics of grammar and punctuation, Max wanted to rewrite it, but I persuaded him to leave it as it was. I was afraid that if I let him doctor it, he'd kill the child whose story it was, and leave me with just the confused adult.

What happened to you after you left Ohura, Max? Ani advised me to talk to Pete or Lily. Does that mean she doesn't know what happened? Or does she just not want to talk about it?

I look down at Max's messy handwriting. That last sentence, things wouldve been different if Id stayed in Ohura, flashes at me like the light on my telephone. Max's narratives are full of these stark statements. Once you're a patched member you're marked for life, he wrote about gang life. These mini-confessions jump out from the middle of an amusing bit of trivia. Which is what I go on to read now — two pages about a girl called Peggy, whom he describes as all right for a sheila. Max was barely six years old when he met Peggy. Was it possible he had an eye for a pretty girl even then?

That girl at the tangi who wept so violently, she was pretty in a destroyed sort of way. I asked Queenie about her, but she didn't even know her name. 'Max is his father's son,' she said. It was the only time I heard her bitter. 'Show him a pretty woman, and he's off like a dog after a rabbit.'

She talked about him as if he were still alive. We all did, I realise now. We still do.

I dunnow how long I lived with my Nan. Time is something I try not to think about. I mean Im banged up in here for 10 years. Well 5 if I keep my nose clean. If I thought about that Id go mad. I did once. Set fire to my mattress. Thats what happens if you think about time and it being real.

The thing about living with Nan is that its never stopped. I think about her every day. So it just goes on if you see what I mean. Sometimes when Ive had a smoke or two it goes on right in front of me. I see and hear things just as if I was back in her house. What does it matter how many weeks or months I was there? Its eternal thats what I rekon. Like Im still sitting in her kitchen listening to her read. Or shes making me read forcing me to break the big words up into silabills then guess what they mean.

If I ever stop seeing those things I rekon Ill be dead.

But there was one thing about Nan I didnt like and that was her coff. It scared me. It was like she had an animal inside her that was trying to get out. Frog in my throat shed say when the spasim was over. She was always talking like that. Raining cats and dogs. A bird in hand. Black dog on your back. Cat got your tongue. I rekon she saw things other people didnt. Or couldnt. The early bird catches the worm shed say when she woke me in the mornings. If I didnt get up straight away shed call me a lazybones and kuff me across the ear. Other days Id be her duck or her little champion her voice going up and down like it was on a seasaw.

But I didnt like the coffing. I asked Ganda about it once and he told me it was the cigaretes. Only he didn't call them cigaretes he called them lungbusters.

They dont make you coff I said to him. I wouldnt have cared if it was him with the animal in his throat.

Dont you go copying your old Nan now will you Max she used to say to me. Cigaretes is bad for you.

Then why dont you throw them away?

If only I could she said.

Nan died in the middle of the night. Shed been coffing so bad Id put my head under the blankets to drown out the noise. Then I heard the door open and Ganda who hardly ever spoke a word to me told me to get dressed and go and find the doktor. And hurry up about it boy he said. Your Nans crook.

I pulled on coat and shoes and ran outside. The sky was so big it scared me. It was the colour of Nans bloomers only instead of holes there were stars. I could hear things too. Snuffly noises like the sky was crying or the stars.

The doktor was Mrs Hollands husband. I knew where he lived. I started shouting before I got to his gate. Come quick my Nans sick. If Nan couldve heard me shed have said youre a poet and you dont know it. She was always saying things like that.

Doktor Holland didnt say anything. Just picked up a funny shaped bag and marched out the door. I went to follow him but Mrs Holland told me to wait for her. In the end we walked back together. She held my hand tight all the way.

No one told me Nan had died. Ganda just sat in his chair and wouldnt talk to anyone. Doktor Holland patted me on the head and told me to be brave. Something fuckwitted like that. Mrs Holland was better. She told me I wouldnt have to go to school in the morning.

The next day all these people came. Auntie Petula she was the first. She was wearing a reath of kawakawa leaves in her hair. It made her look like shed just jumped out of a birds nest. She told me Nan was going to have a proper tangi. Shed spoken to the kaumatua. It was all agreed. It didnt matter that Nan was Pakeha. Shed been a good wife the best. Now that Nan was dead she wasnt going to let that lazy bastard brother of hers screw things up the way he had when Nan was alive. Only she didn't call her Nan she called her Violet. That was her name see.

58

Hot on the heels of Auntie Petula came all these other people. Truckloads of them. Most of the women had birds nest hairdos too. They had to wait outside till Auntie Petula came out on the porch waving a green branch around and wailing like a cat. I thought it was weird especially when I saw what theyd done to Nan. Put her in this open coffin with flowers piled at her feet. Of course I know what was going on now. Ive learned my Maoritanga. But then was diferent. I might as well have been watching a performance by Marshans for all the sense it made.

What Auntie Petula was doing was calling people on to the marae. Thats what Nans house had been turned into see. A marae. The strange noise she made was called a karanga. It was to welcome people to the wharemate the house of death.

Haere mai ra e te iwi e,
Maurui mai te aroha ki tenei a tatou
Kua tiraha atu i te ra nei
Haere mai, haere mai!
Welcome people
Bring your compassion to this one of us
Who lies here today
Welcome, welcome!

It was hard to believe Auntie Petula was Gandas sister. She was half his size for starters. But she had Ganda sorted and no mistake. He was to sit beside the cofin and he wasnt to move. He wasnt to be given any beer either. Sober the old goat up whether he likes it or not I heard her say.

Nans feet were pointing towards the door so that her spirit could find its way out to begin its journey to the underworld. I didnt know that then. I wish I had. I might have hung round a bit longer.

During a lull in the proceedings I heard Auntie Petula say to one of the cuzzies (all the people who came seemed to be cuzzies) that Ganda wasnt fit to look after a goldfish. And someone else one of her daughters I think say there was no way that kids going back to Queenies. I knew they meant me when they said that kid. They must have thought I was fuckwitted or deaf talking about me while I was standing there.

Its only now I see how weird it was that Queenie didnt come down for the tangi. I mean Nan was her mother. Sam the Sadist surely wouldnt have stopped her going to her own mothers tangi. Or maybe he would. Anythings possible with that piece of deadmeat. If Id hung round a bit longer I might have found out but thats like saying if Id been born to a different family Id have had a better life. Waste of time thinking like that.

My friend Peggy came round with her mum but they didnt come into the house. Peggys mum said that was for Maori. Peggy handed me this cake and her mum said she was sorry for my loss.

There were other people hanging about outside too. Pakeha. The family next door brung a box of vegtables and a farmer from outside Ohura brung a great hunk of meat.

But the doktor and Mrs Holland didnt hang about. They waited till some more cuzzies drove up then they followed Auntie Petula into the house. They didnt seem to mind that the place was full of dead people. Because it was. I know that now.

Ei whakataukia mai ra te rangi o te mamae e

Kia tutaki mai nga mate kau pa ki ahau!

Bring the song of pain and lay it down

So my dead may gather round me!

Mrs Holland and her husband even hongied with Ganda and the cuzzies as if theyd been doing it all their lives.

And all the time Nan lay in that cofin not saying anything not talking about birds or cats or frogs not even coffing.

At the end of the day Auntie Petula called everyone to the wharekai which was really just the shed out the back for a feed. That was when I knew what I was going to do. Id promised Nan I wouldnt do a runner but Nan wasnt here any more so my promise didnt count. Not everyone went out for kai. Ganda wasnt allowed to leave Nan. That could have spelt trouble for me but luckily the old rooster was so dozey he wouldnt have noticed if Id nicked something out of his pocket.

What I did was this. When there was only Ganda and me left in the house I went to the chair he usually sat in and squeezed my hand down the side. I pulled out an envelop opened it and found 3 twenty dollar notes. I rekoned that was a sign.

I stuffed the money into my trouser pocket put the envelop back grabbed my coat and walked out the door. It didnt matter that it was dark or that the sky was still crying. I knew the road I wanted. It was the one that would take me as far as I could get from Auckland.

9

Greg stayed in London three and a half weeks. Towards the end of that time he asked me to come back to New Zealand with him. I can't pretend the question came as a surprise. When a man tells you repeatedly that you are beautiful, that he adores you, that you are the woman he should always have been with, asking you to make a life with him can hardly be described as a sudden move. There was of course no question of him making a life with me. Even if his work were not based in New Zealand, his passionate commitment for his country ruled out any possibility of an alternative.

'I know you *want* to come back,' he said. 'You've as good as said so. And don't tell me you're happy here because I can see you're not.'

'I've lived here fifteen years, Greg. It's my home now.'

'You're a New Zealander.'

'My work is here.'

'What work? Teaching people how to write? That's a waste of time, and you know it.'

'I was meaning my own writing.'

A smug expression settled on Greg's face. 'But you haven't published a novel in, what? Five years?' he accused. 'Don't you think you might do better in New Zealand?'

'The reason I haven't published is . . .'

'Are you afraid to come back, is that it? Fifteen years, and not one visit.'

'I could visit you,' I suggested brightly. 'Then we could see . . .'

Greg turned away from me. Something in the way he was holding himself, back ramrod straight, arms folded across his chest, told me the argument was closed. It was my first experience of Greg's uncanny ability to bring me to a point where I no longer knew what I thought or felt; then make plain by his silence that our discussion was ended. It's a technique I've seen him use to good effect in court, creating in his opponent a sense of unease which leads, almost invariably, to a climb-down. But I had no counsel to defend me. I was in love with Greg. The dam I had built around my heart had been breached. When Greg put me outside the circle of his love, as he did on that, and on many subsequent occasions, I could barely control my panic. How could someone who 'adored' me, who placed me above all other women, become a stranger in the space of a few seconds? I *had* to get him to turn his head. I had to get him to touch me.

That first time reconciliation came quickly. Later it could take as long as a month. 'I promise I'll come before Christmas,' I said, sliding my arms round his back and pulling him to me. 'I'll base myself with you, and make lightning trips to see my mother. You're right. I should never have stayed away so long.'

He didn't answer straightaway. But as I went on murmuring my love for him, I felt the tension leave his body. 'Once you've seen where I live,' he said, turning back to me, 'you won't miss England at all.'

'Just because you don't like London . . .'

'My house is on a cliff overlooking the Waitemata. It was built before the First World War as part of a large estate. Most of the land's been sold now, but it's surrounded by bush, and so quiet you'd never guess you were living close to the centre of the country's largest city. You'll wake to the sound of tui, and fall asleep to the cries of moreporks. You'll be able to write without the shriek of traffic in your ears, and you won't have to wear half a dozen jerseys to keep warm . . .'

By the time he stopped talking I was once again in a state of enchantment. Two months later I walked through the door of the house he had described so eloquently. To say my spirits sank the moment I stepped over the threshold is a cliché, but that is exactly what happened. Dark panelled walls; dusty antique furniture; sash windows smeared with dirt; faded curtains laced with cobwebs; an antediluvian kitchen with a cooker that sloped backwards, as did most things on that side of the house; bathroom walls speckled with mould; taps that groaned when you turned them on; a living room so gloomy it needed the light turned on in the middle of the day; a dead rat in the pantry. Oblivious to my reaction, Greg took me on a tour of the house, and what he euphemistically called the 'garden', directing my eye to the harbour view, and my ear to the discordant chatter of rosellas. At the end of the tour I reminded Greg of the words he wrote to me before I left London. 'You promised you'd sell the house if I didn't like it,' I recalled. 'Did you mean that?'

'You haven't agreed to live with me yet.'

'But if I did . . .'

He grinned. 'Let's talk about it in bed,' he said.

10

That first spring and summer, visiting Max in prison, encouraging him to write, I came to realise something about my own life. Something so fundamental that for months I denied what was happening, and simply went on in the old way, as if Max and the experience of prison had nothing to teach me.

'Fiction is about reality,' I used to say to him, repeating a phrase I'd used before, in very different circumstances. 'It isn't the same as reality, but it's connected to it, sometimes by no more than a thin thread. But connected it must be. You could say fiction is reality *heightened*.'

I don't know how much Max understood, or even cared, about what I was saying, but I didn't want him thinking I, as his teacher, was by definition a better writer. I'd simply had more practice, that was all. I was knowing and self-conscious and clever. I could write to order. I'd had to, to survive in Britain: adapting novels for television and radio; producing outlines calculated to win me publishing commissions; mining my contemporaries for clues as to what made a novel successful.

Max, just by being who he was, taught me to despise all that. For him writing was, almost literally, a matter of life and death. If he didn't get his stories out into the light, the darkness would overwhelm him and he would die.

It took a near tragedy to remove the scales from my eyes. Summer was coming to an end when the prison phoned to say all Max's privileges had been removed for two months. Since my visits came under the heading of privileges, I wouldn't see him again till the autumn. But that particular punishment was only the tip of the iceberg. For the first week, Max would be put in the pound, a place even the toughest inmates feared, then he would be locked in his cell for twenty-three hours a day till the end of his sentence. When I asked what he had done to deserve such treatment, I was told he'd threatened a warder. Instinctively I knew which warder — the Belfast bully I'd encountered on my first visit.

Shortly after that phone call I received a letter from Max. In it he told me he'd done nothing to provoke the warder, he'd merely asked if he was entitled to a new phonecard. Despite the fact that by then I knew Max to be as capable of lying as he was of the sudden, deadly insult, I chose to believe him. Unfortunately the authorities chose to believe the warder.

'It's barbaric,' I complained bitterly to Greg. 'What possible good can it do to lock a man up like that? I don't care what he's done . . .'

'Don't you?'

'He didn't hit anybody.'

'Not this time, no.'

'I've heard *you* say some pretty insulting things to people. Well, *about* people mostly, but still . . .'

'I'm not a criminal, Renate. That's the difference.'

In the weeks that followed I couldn't stop thinking about Max, locked in his cell, denied his books for all I knew, allowed only one sheet of paper to write his weekly letter. What would he do with himself? What dark places would his thoughts take him to?

Six weeks into his sentence I received another phone call. Max had tried to hang himself with strips of cotton torn from his mattress. Would I be prepared to resume my visits while an enquiry was under way? I was too shocked to ask the right questions. All I could do was agree, and wait for Saturday to come.

'Great way to get attention,' Greg reacted, when I told him.

'Men have killed themselves in Pare before,' I reminded him sharply.

'Yes, and they will again, no doubt.'

I couldn't get Greg's words out of my mind. Driving to the prison they played over and over in my head, infuriating me with their persistence. Even if Max's attempt to kill himself wasn't serious, but a cry for help, how could Greg dismiss it so casually? He was a criminal lawyer, known for his support of the Howard League for Penal Reform. Wasn't even a failed attempt at suicide proof that something was terribly wrong?

'You're the one teaching Maxwell Nene, aren't you?' the warder asked, as I emptied the contents of my bag onto her desk. I was relieved not to be faced with the usual harpy. This warder, a pleasant-faced woman with a Newcastle accent, was new.

'That's right.'

'He got a rum deal,' she confided, lowering her voice so only I would hear. 'There are people in here who've got it in for him.'

'Why? Because of what he's done? Or supposed to have done?'

'You don't have to *do* anything, pet. It's enough just to be who you are . . . You know he tried to hang himself?' she added, when she'd finished with my bag.

I nodded. I was beginning to feel like a criminal myself, eyes darting to right and left, looking to see where the next betrayal might come from.

'That's why you're here,' the warder explained. 'They figure you might save them some aggro.'

Minutes later I was holding Max in my arms. We always hugged on meeting, but this was different. Some kind of exchange was going on, his reality — the prevailing dark of his world — for the life *I* represented, the life of words.

'They told you then,' he said, when we'd released our grip.

I nodded.

'Go on,' he grinned. 'Tell me I'm a dickhead.'

'You're a dickhead,' I muttered.

'Won't happen again. Promise.'

'Like you promised your Nan you wouldn't do a runner?'

'This is different.'

'Oh?'

'There's you and me now.'

'There was you and me before this happened.'

'Yeah but . . .'

'I'm your teacher, Max. And I'm your friend. But I can't stop you . . .'

'Hey, Renate. Nunna that. You don't want them to put me on a charge again, do you?'

'I'm not crying.'

'Got a cold, that it?'

'Something like that.'

He took my hand then, and led me through the visiting room to the yard. It was one of those soft autumn days, warm, without a trace of humidity, when if I closed my eyes I could believe I was back in England. We found a place near the door and positioned our chairs so the sun shone on our backs.

I don't think I'd ever been so aware of Max's tattoos before. He was wearing shorts and a T-shirt. His arms and legs were a mass of blue blobs, some recognisable — a tiki, a large spider, a taiaha — others, resembling a web of intersecting railway lines, unidentifiable. Max had several times promised to tell me the stories behind his tattoos, but the only ones I ever succeeded in getting him to talk about were the ones on his cheeks, acquired during his first lag in prison. What *was* recognisable were the gang insignia. The word PATU was blazoned across the backs of his hands, advertising his former affiliation for everyone to see.

'I've been reading the Psalms,' Max announced, when we were seated. 'That's all they'd let me have, the *Bible*.'

'I was afraid of that.'

'Don't be. It was great. The guys who wrote that stuff, they knew what it was like to feel the shit comin' down. *'It was no enemy that taunted me,'* he quoted. *'Or I should have avoided him; No foe that treated me with scorn, Or I should have kept out of his way. It was you, a man of my own sort . . .'*

He didn't seem to notice I was incapable of responding. I

hadn't seen him for nearly two months. Now, sitting beside me, three days after his brush with death, he was so powerfully, physically, *there*, I was stunned into silence.

'*They wear their pride like a necklace, And violence like a robe that wraps them round . . .*'

His words came at me fast, in the countertenor-ish voice he used when excited. I interrupted him only once, to express my amazement at how much he'd committed to memory. He dismissed my praise with a flick of his head, as if the effort of memorizing were of no significance at all. It was the content he wanted to impress on me: his identification with the proud, passionate, homeless people of the Psalms.

'*I am a passing guest as all my forefathers were,*' he recited, towards the end of his *tour de force*. '*Frown on me no more and let me smile again, Before I go away and cease to be.*'

It was those words that most affected me. It was as if Max had accepted, at his tender age, the imminent approach of death. The thought so alarmed me I found myself looking round for help, like the Psalmist lifting his eyes to the hills. But in that dark place there was no help for anyone.

'Do you ever hate yourself, Renate?' he asked me, when he'd run out of lines to quote. 'I mean, really hate yourself, so that you're eaten up with shame.'

'Of course,' I answered. 'Doesn't everyone?'

'I'm not talking about twinges of conscience. I'm talkin' about the kinda shame that makes you puke in your bed at night. You wouldn't know about that. How could you?'

I tried to argue with him, but I got nowhere. I'd seen him in this mood before. He didn't want me to answer his questions. He wanted to shift the burden of what he was feeling on to my shoulders. Everything he said came with a sting in the tail. My life, he reminded me, in a dozen different ways, was as unlike his as a duke's was to a dustman's. I had been born with a silver spoon in my mouth. He came into this world with a chain around his neck and a curse on his name.

Perhaps I should have interrupted him; insisted he hear my

story, instead of second-guessing it. If I'd told him about my life in England and what happened to me there, it might have stemmed the flow of disgusted self-pity. There's a limit to how many ways you can complain about the arbitrary nature of birth, and the meaninglessness of life.

'So it's all down to chance, is it?' I asked, when he paused long enough for me to speak.

'Chance?' Max queried.

'Your birth. Your name. The fact that you're here.'

'Leave it out, Renate,' he muttered.

'You told me once that the fact you were busted was just bad luck. Which means it was *good* luck someone looked into your cell the other night. Luck and chance, they're the same thing, aren't they?'

Max frowned, chewed the nail of his thumb, then laughed, in one of his mercurial changes of mood. 'Chance. Yeah,' he said. 'I bet you a million dollars there's more guilty men walking round outside these walls than there are in the whole prison system. So those of us who are inside are here by chance. Yeah. I believe that. Sure. Do you?'

'I don't know, Max. I don't know what to believe any more.'

Later, as we queued for coffee, Max asked me if I'd remembered his cigarette papers.

'What cigarette papers?'

'I wrote to you about them.'

'The only letter I've had from you was the one you wrote at the beginning of all this.'

'Bastards!' Max muttered.

Driving home that day, replaying everything Max had said, fighting the suspicion that he deliberately created confusion in order to retain the upper hand, I acknowledged for the first time that being with Max, visiting him in prison, had changed my life. And not just my life, my work. In those moments of clarity I understood that the novel I'd been working on for the last six months was no good. There was nothing intrinsically wrong with it. It was shaping up to be a well-told story in the tradition of social realism. Like my two previous novels it was set in New Zealand, a departure from my earlier work, most of which had been set in England. It's even true I'd been enjoying the writing. Rediscovering my native country as I moved the narrative from a Canterbury sheep station to a suburban villa in Auckland, then back to the South Island, to the small town of Oamaru, had been yielding unexpected pleasures. But it wouldn't do. Those were the words hammering in my brain as I struggled to make sense of Max's life. Compared to what had happened to him, it just wasn't important. Nothing about it was inevitable.

'Your publisher won't like it,' Greg pointed out reasonably, when I announced my decision. 'I'm not sure anyone will. What's brought this on anyway? You were going great guns last time we spoke.'

'It's hard to explain . . .'

'Nothing to do with Maxwell Nene, is it?'

'No . . .'

'You don't sound very sure.'

'I told you, I can't explain.'

'You know, I worry about you, Renate,' Greg said. 'Every time you go to the prison you come back with some harebrained idea.' He paused to position a fresh cigarette in his holder. Then he sat back in his chair and contemplated me through a curl of smoke. 'I wonder sometimes if you know who you are.'

11

Strange that it should have been my life in London — the part of it I shared with Cecil — that haunted me through the long afternoon at Greg's bedside. Strange because I would have described my marriage to Greg as deeply committed, at least on my side, whereas Cecil and I were neither married nor, in any conventional sense, committed. Leaving each other free was our — or rather, if I'm honest, *my* — rule of thumb. Letting love and only love be our guide. So why didn't the ghost of my life with Greg put in an appearance? It had been messing up my psyche for most of the last two years. And there, beside me, was its embodiment. It didn't make sense. I hadn't thought about Cecil, not consciously, for weeks.

'OK,' I addressed his shade, 'so what's all this about then? And don't tell me Max sent you. Max didn't even know your name.'

That name. It was the first intimate thing I learned about him. It could have been the last! 'Cecil!' I shrieked, in a moment of involuntary rudeness. The man standing before me in no way matched my image of a Cecil. This flesh and blood incarnation was wearing ill-fitting trousers, ancient leather sandals and a loose cotton jacket that looked like a leftover from the Chinese revolution. In no way did he resemble the monocled, velvet-jacketed creature of my imagination. 'You're joking,' I finished lamely.

'Afraid not,' he answered.

My embarrassment was total. Cecil was my GP. I'd been

coming to him for six months. In so far as I'd imagined his name at all, I'd thought of him as a Matthew or a Sebastian. This particular visit was about a boil on my neck. A more unlikely start to a romance could not be imagined.

I suppose, if we were to meet in this way today, as doctor and patient, our friendship would be doomed. But back then, in the permissive seventies, eyebrows did not automatically rise at the prospect of a doctor dating a patient. Though Cecil was quick to insist, once our friendship became intimate, that I change to another practice. Against my will, I might add. Cecil was an excellent GP.

'Don't you have another name?' I asked him, when I'd got to know him better. 'A middle name or something.'

'John,' he told me. 'But that's not the point.'

'Why not? You've just admitted you don't like the name. You could have changed it. Saved yourself a lot of misery.'

'I thought about it. I thought about it a lot. But every time I tried to imagine myself as John it felt wrong. Besides, I was named after an uncle, a favourite uncle as it happens.'

'So you're stuck with it then.'

He grinned, tossing his head to get rid of the hair in his eyes. This was the hirsute seventies, remember. Cecil wasn't the only man who walked round looking like Jesus.

In the end I got used to the name myself. 'I love you, Cecil,' I'd murmur, leaning into his bony shoulder. 'And if you go on treating me so well I probably always will.'

'What are you doing here?' I demanded, seeing Cecil's ghost had taken up what looked like permanent residence on the other side of the room. I glanced at Greg's inert body. Neither dead nor alive, he far more than I belonged in the twilight world of apparitions and hauntings. Greg and I never really talked about Cecil. He was no threat to us: at first I assumed that was the reason, but as I got to know Greg better I began to realise he was just uninterested. Anything going on in my current life — Max in particular — was of great interest to him; but the past, especially my English past, aroused no curiosity.

'Why didn't you marry the guy?' he asked, on one of the few occasions Cecil's name came up. 'Since he was such a saint.'

'I never said he was a saint.'

'All that unpaid work for his patients. His utter devotion to you. Though of course I've only your word for that. I'd call that saintly, wouldn't you?'

'It's normal behaviour for some people,' I retaliated.

Just for a moment I was tempted to remind Greg of those words. But he, lying passively beside me, seemed even less alive than Cecil.

I could sense Cecil smiling at me. For some reason it made me think of my father, who smiled right at me just minutes before he died. 'I'll tell you something, Renate,' Dad said, or rather mouthed, since his voice had almost gone by then. 'I'm looking forward to the company of the dead. Imagine being able to chat with Tolstoy.'

I would have been happy for my father to haunt me every day of my life. He died when I was twelve, when I was still unashamedly in love with him, so I'd have welcomed his ghost. Instead I had to wait for Max to die to experience a haunting. First Max and then Cecil. Two ghosts in as many weeks.

'Don't you have a voice?' I complained. 'At least Max talks to me.'

'Bloody key doesn't fit,' Cecil said, catapulting me back twenty-two years to our first holiday, in Cornwall.

Instinctively I put my hands to my ears. I didn't want to hear those words. I didn't want to be reminded. But Cecil was impervious to my distress. 'We can always sleep in the car I suppose,' he said hopefully.

We'd just driven down from London. Six hours of fuggy happiness in Cecil's old Wolseley. A night-time journey, to give us as many hours together as possible. Now we were at our destination, a cliff-side cottage belonging to friends of Cecil's. Only we couldn't open the door.

'In this weather?' I answered him. 'We'd be blocks of ice by morning.'

We had been lovers for a month. We couldn't seem to get enough of each other. Which was why we'd come to Cornwall. Two weeks to do exactly as we pleased.

We peered into the darkness, searching for a lighted window. There were half a dozen other cottages, scattered over the headland like abandoned toys. But the only light we could see, apart from the intermittent flash from the lighthouse, was the milky gleam of the sea, so pale, in the absence of moon and stars, as to seem an illusion.

'Don't suppose you brought a torch,' Cecil said.

'It's your car, darling.'

'Right. But you're the practical one.'

We giggled conspiratorially.

'What time is it?' I asked.

'Can't see without a torch.'

Cecil pinned his hair behind his ears, and tried the key again. 'Come on,' he urged. 'Please don't do this to me.' A noise like the rustling of silk was followed by a whistle of triumph. 'Eureka!' he exclaimed, turning a glowing face to me. 'Welcome to paradise!'

It was not just my ears I wanted to cover then, but my eyes. If I let myself walk in through that door, if I saw the sitting room with its tiny fireplace and the basket filled with wood sitting on the grate; if I passed on through the heavy oak door to the bedroom with its narrow bed covered with a patchwork quilt, I wouldn't get through the afternoon. I was in the hospital to watch over Greg, not mourn a man I still can't think about without pain . . .

When I first met Cecil I wasn't attracted to him. He wasn't my type. He was tall, spectacularly freckled, painfully shortsighted and inclined to bump into the furniture, even when wearing glasses. He dressed badly, wore his hair long and smoked whenever and wherever he could. That his hair was the colour of rust was a further mark against him, but all that ceased to matter once we became lovers. It was as if, in a single touch of his lips, all my preconceived notions about love had been demolished. 'I can't seem to get enough of you,' I said to him, at the end of our first week, when little else existed for me but our snatched moments of bliss.

'Ditto,' he answered. 'So what do you say we take some time off? There's a cottage I can get hold of in Cornwall . . .'

The more I tried not to go through the door of that cliff-side cottage, the more persistent the images became. So I tried a different tactic. Every half hour or so a nurse looked in on Greg. If I kept my eye fixed on the light coming from the passage, Cecil, lounging nonchalantly on the other side of the room, would disappear. Better still, if I talked aloud to Greg, the voices in my head would be forced to stay silent.

'I never really told you how I felt about Cecil, did I?' I said, laying down my challenge to the unconscious figure beside me. 'Because I absolutely adored him. He was the most beautiful man I've ever known. He had one of those complexions that would have been destroyed by our southern sun: long, straight auburn hair; freckles over ninety per cent of his body. I used to tell him he looked like a pointillist painting . . . And you were right, you know. He *was* a sort of saint. His ambitions were all to do with other people: getting a sick child back on his feet; making his depressed mother smile again; seeing my books in print. My mistake was that I didn't realise how rare he was. I'd had boyfriends before, of course, but this was the first time I'd been in love. I assumed it was the being in love that made everything so nearly perfect, whereas it wasn't, it was Cecil himself. Because when I fell in love with you . . .'

I stopped. Something had got stuck in my throat. As I peered at Greg's face I realised what it was. It was anger. 'Can you hear what I'm saying, Greg? No one really knows what goes on when you're in a coma. You should have wanted to know how it was between me and Cecil. You shouldn't have looked bored when I tried to tell you.'

I took in a long breath; held it for a count of ten. There was no point being angry. Not now, not here. Cecil would tell me to get a grip on myself, see things in proportion.

I turned round, expecting Cecil to have vanished, but he was still there, one elbow resting on the windowsill, his long skinny body curved seductively against the wall. Women are supposed to be the seductive ones, but no one could be with Cecil for long without observing the effect he had on the opposite sex. It used to worry me, till I realised he was that rare breed, a completely faithful man. Well, maybe not completely. Under pressure he would admit to finding other women attractive. But miraculous though it still seems to me, I was the woman he wanted.

So why didn't we marry? 'Why didn't we marry?' I demanded of Cecil's ghost. Though of course I knew why, and so did he. We didn't even live together. I kept my flat in the Fulham Road, he kept his in Edith Grove. 'We live so close,' we agreed happily, at the beginning. 'We can spend as much time together as we want.'

'Oh go away, Cecil, please,' I pleaded. 'This isn't helping.'

But Cecil remained impervious. As I glanced back at Greg an explosion of sound filled the room: waves crashing on rocks; surf pounding; the wild shrieking of gulls. I recognised those gulls. They weren't the ordinary English variety, but the fierce companions of shipwrecks and drowning men that haunt the coasts of Cornwall. 'No,' I groaned, looking back at my tormentor, 'I won't remember. You can't make me.'

But of course he could, and did. Eight winters in succession we holidayed in that grey stone cottage on the edge of the cliff. Once the home of a coastguard, it became a place of indescribable joy for us. By day we roamed the rocky inlets and fierce, seaweed-infested beaches, gathering sea spinach and pennywort for our supper; scrambling down bracken-tangled paths in search of smugglers' caves; crouching behind skeletal trees, bent like pipe cleaners against the wind, to light Cecil's cigarettes. The fact that this was a dangerous landscape, subject to sudden erosion, added to our sense of excitement. Hunting for signs of drowned farmland and buried cottages became part of each day's adventure.

By night we sat around a fire that spat out resin and scorched our faces, drinking beer, eating the fish we'd bought that day on the wharf at Looe, counting the seconds between the flashes from the lighthouse. We'd take our time because we knew what riches lay ahead for us when the meal was over. 'I'm going to start at your feet,' I would tease. 'Then move slowly up your body till every freckle has been kissed.'

I don't understand why such happiness had to end. Or was that what you came to tell me, Cecil? That it hasn't ended. It's changed into something else. But if that's the case then Greg, Greg and me, we haven't ended either. Which, presumably, is why I'm sitting here.

I took Greg's lifeless hand in mine. 'Just get better,' I ordered, the words burning a hole in my throat. 'I'll leave you alone then.'

I turned round to find Cecil gone. In his place stood Max. In the bright hospital light he looked yellow rather than brown. He shook his body, as if adjusting to his new surroundings, then he grinned at me. 'That was interesting,' he said.

'What are *you* doing here?'

'Queenie's been asking for you.'

'Oh?'

'She's got something to tell you.'

'Fat lot you care.'

'I got rid of Cecil for you, didn't I?'

'So you know his name?'

'I do now.'

'Why are you here, Max?'

'I told you. I'm getting sorted.'

'And I'm supposed to help with that, am I?'

'We help each other. That's always been the deal.'

'But it's different now,' I protested. 'You're dead. Why did that happen, Max? Was it because I wouldn't lend you my car? Because if that was the reason . . .'

I stopped, aware that Cecil was listening, even if I couldn't see him. 'Sometimes Max, just sometimes,' I muttered in my own defence, 'you push people too far . . . It's easy for you to dismiss me as a materialistic Pakeha, isn't it? Too easy. *You* weren't averse to a few home comforts, as I remember . . . I needed the car that weekend anyway . . .'

'Did I say any of that?' Max's voice was full of laughter. Up to his old tricks, I remember thinking. 'Those are your words, not mine,' he said.

'I can't help you, Max. You'll have to get sorted without me.'

I turned to the door, willing the nurse to appear. There had to be something I could take to stop hallucinations. A pill or potion of some kind.

It was at that moment I was struck by a chilling thought. I didn't understand love at all. In all probability I'd never understood it. Look at the mess I'd made of things with Cecil, followed a decade later by the collapse of my marriage to Greg. Some of that *had* to be down to me. And then there was Max; *is* Max, since he's clearly intent on haunting me. I loved him, many of us loved him; but it wasn't enough. He still died. What would Cecil have done if he'd been me? Would he have behaved any differently?

'You've turned me into a cynic,' I accused, peering over my shoulder at Greg.

'Cut that out, Renate,' Max admonished.

'You're still there then,' I said, turning my head reluctantly.

'You'll be blaming Greg for my death next.'

'And what if I do?'

'It's not the answer. You know that.'

'Perhaps we should have had you on a suicide watch,' I muttered. 'You were a child, a tattooed, criminal child. We should never have expected you to behave like an adult.'

Max's laugh, in that echoing room, sounded shocking.

'You've hurt so many people,' I threw back at him. 'Did you have to do that? There's Ani and Pete, and Queenie whose pain I'll no doubt see for myself when I visit her. And there's no need to grin at me like that. You know perfectly well I'll go and see her. Oh, and while we're on the subject, who was that girl at the tangi? Why was she crying so much? You never told me you had a girlfriend. If that's what she was. No one else seemed to know her. Walter called her a tart . . .'

I sat back, confident my words would have breached his defences. But he just went on grinning at me. 'Nothing to say? Typical. You're a bloody convolvulus root, Max. Ani's right.'

Angry now, I turned away again. Where *was* that nurse? I needed her, even if Greg didn't. 'You can laugh all you like,' I said, tossing the words back at Max. 'Don't let me stop you. Must be highly amusing watching me in this state. Talking to myself. Seeing things that aren't there. It would never occur to you, I suppose, to help me. That would spoil your fun.'

I turned back to the window, ready to do battle, but Max was gone. The room was bright and hot and empty.

After what seemed many minutes I turned back to Greg. For the first time I let myself feel the pain of that altered, no longer handsome face. Something hard rose in my throat, but it wasn't anger this time, it was grief. I gasped, and fell forward onto the bed. That was when I heard the gulls again. Not loud and clear, as before, but faint and far away, like a siren heard through sleep.

'It's not finished, Renate,' Cecil whispered in my ear. 'It won't be finished until . . .'

But the rest of the sentence, if he ever spoke it, was lost.

12

I joined the gang when I was twelve. I'd been living in this Boy's Home in Rotorua but on my twelfth birthday I did a bunk. I reckoned they had it coming to them. Not that they were all bad but there was this one bloke, Andy Fairweather. Randy Andy we christened him when he appeared on the horizon (you can tell that sort a mile off), and it was him, when I clocked what was happening, that he was about to come on to me, that I ran away from.

Getting picked up by the gang was the best thing that could have happened to me. Then. I'm not saying it's good now. But then was different. Another planet.

Running away wasn't a first for me. I'd shot through a few times before. My best escape, the one I skited about the most, was from this foster home the Social put me in. Don't remember how old I was. Nine or ten I reckon.

My foster parents (Parents! Ha!) were called Mr and Mrs McAlistair. They had six pink-faced progeny of their own. The six little pigs, I called them, only they weren't so little. God knows how I got stuck with that gang of trainee skinheads. Far as they were concerned, and I'm talking about the whole bloody lot of them, Mr and Mrs Hitler included, I was a dirty hori, not fit to breathe the same air as them. You could smell the hatred on them even when they weren't bashing the living daylights out of me or calling me a kumera cruncher. Maybe the Social thought they'd lick some sense into me. I'd run away from one foster home already. Or maybe they just hoped I'd turn into a potato, brown on the outside, white on the inside. That's the kinda Maori they like.

'You're a filthy little brat,' Mrs McAlistair used to hiss at me during the morning inspection of ears and fingernails. 'God knows what you do in the bathroom but it's sure as eggs not washing.'

This would bring on a spurt of giggling from the younger little pigs, soon silenced by their mother. 'It's no laughing matter,' she'd snap. 'Cleanliness is next to godliness. The reason I'm angry with Maxwell is because he refuses to mend his ways. Such arrogance puts him in the Devil's camp.'

I don't know whether it was those words, or others like it which she bandied about on a daily basis, but the older kids seemed to feel they could do what they liked to me. I was regularly set on after school, sometimes by the whole pack of them. If anything the girls were worse than the boys. 'Hey! There's the coconut!' they'd shout, as they came round the corner. As the boys began to lash out with fists and boots, they'd chorus encouragement. 'Give it to him Wayne! Bet he's got black blood just like his black heart. Oh look, he's blubbing. Does the poor little bubby want his mother?'

Other times, when it was just the girls, they'd throw stones and call me a dork or a dumb-bum. I'd shout back that thing my Nan taught me, 'Sticks and stones may break my bones but names'll never do it.' But that only made them worse.

Till one day Wayne, the eldest, told me my mother had come to see me at the school but she'd been sent away. I didn't believe him at first. But then he said how she had this tattoo on her chin and a limp when she walked. I knew then it was Queenie.

I could read Wayne pretty well by this time. I could always tell when he was lying. So when I asked him why my mother had been sent away, and he told me, I knew it was the truth. 'She was drunk,' he said, laughing in my face. 'Staggering about like a headless chook. Wish you coulda seen it, Dozo. Funny as a fit.'

If I'd hit Wayne then I'd probably have killed him. He was bigger than me but he was a sook. I could have flattened him, no trouble. But I had a better idea. I'd go back to the house and pack my gear and take to the road. With luck I'd find my way to Queenie's place. She wouldn't have come looking for me if the coast hadn't been clear.

But where I ended up, after some stuff I don't wanna write about, was a Boy's Home. Not the one in Rotorua. That came later. This one was in Auckland somewhere. Queenie came to see me a few times. She told me she wanted me back but the Social weren't having it. On her last visit she told me about Will Walsh. She said he was OK, but I didn't believe her. She'd said that before, about Sam the Sadist. So I did another bunk, lived rough for a few weeks, and ended up in Rotorua. I didn't see Queenie no more after that.

Rotorua wasn't too bad at first. Some of the goons in the Home were almost human. But then Randy Andy came on the scene and I knew I had to get outa there. By then running away had become a way of life for me. Not that I went much on living rough but given a choice between Randy Andy and the bush, I'd choose the bush any day.

This was my plan. I'd sneak back from school when Randy and the other goons were having lunch, get my gear together, and head for the hot pools. There was this shed where some of us Maori kids went sometimes for a smoke. I'd be safe there for a day or two till the heat was off. I'd be warm too. The steam coming off them pools was better than a hot shower.

I didn't have any money or food or that but I'd had plenty of practice nicking wallets and that was what I done. Tourists are easy game. Specially when they see you as a cute brown kid, hanging about the shops cause you've got no mother and father. I picked up quite a bit that way, legitimately, if you see what I mean. 'What's your name son?' some hefty Yank with a camera round his neck and a baseball cap jammed on his head, would ask. And I'd turn to his wife, who'd be wearing tartan trousers and sneakers, and I'd open my eyes as wide as they'd go and the bored look would leave her face and she'd smile at me. That was the signal for me to announce I was descended from the warrior Hone Heke, whose quarrel with the British had led to the confiscation of all our lands. 'Do you hear that Emily?' the Yank would bellow, as if what I'd just told him was the secret of the universe. 'That's a real sad story, son,' he'd say to me. And his hand would reach for his wallet. A couple of encounters like that and I'd be set for the day.

I hid out in that shed three days, by which time I figured I better be moving on. I'd only lifted two wallets, one of them useless since the money was foreign, geek money. But two unhappy tourists were enough to get the cops sniffing around.

I was all packed up and ready to go when I spotted some blokes walking slowly towards me through the steam. You had to be careful how you walked in this part of Rotorua. One false step and you could end up in a pool of boiling porridge.

As they got nearer I saw there were four of them, big dudes. Two of them were Maori, but I couldn't tell about the others. They were wearing jeans and leather jackets with badges on them and the meanest boots you ever saw.

The steam was real thick that day. So was the stink. If you've ever smelt a rotten egg then you'll know. Rotorua smells like rotten eggs.

Normally I wouldn't have tried anything on with locals. Specially not ones that looked like these blokes, 'large as life and twice as ugly', as Nan would say. But I reckoned the steam gave me an advantage. Besides, these dudes weren't poor. You only had to look at their boots to know that. They could spare a few dollars.

I sauntered out of my hidey-hole and made out I was looking for something I'd dropped on the pumice. As the first of my targets drew parallel, I called out, 'Kia ora!'

He stopped and stared at me. Fuck! I thought. This is one mean-looking dude. Every bit of his face except his eyes was tattooed. There was even a tattoo on his lips. No way was I going to rob this joker. I was that scared I thought I might fill my pants.

'Hey, Duke!' the dude called over his shoulder. 'Look what we've got here. Real little smart-arse.'

'My name's Max,' I squeaked.

'Gudday Max.'

By this time the four of them were bunched round me like a war party of Indians looking for their next scalp. I was glad of that steam for a different reason now. Hot piss was running down my legs.

'OK Rooster, you've had your fun,' the one called Duke drawled. 'We've got a job to do, remember?'

I hardly dared look at Duke. He was even bigger than Rooster. But he wasn't Maori, least I didn't reckon so. He had tattoos though. All four of them had those.

'What ya doing here, Max?' Rooster asked.

'Looking for my money.'

'Dropped it did ya?'

'Actually I'm running away,' I confessed. It wasn't what I'd meant to say but once the words were out I could hardly call them back. 'From the Boy's Home,' I added desperately. Something about the way all four were staring was really putting the frighteners on me. Any minute now it wouldn't be just rotten eggs you could smell.

What I was thinking as they went on staring was how easy it would be for them to throw me into one of the pools of boiling porridge surrounding us. There was no one about. Even if there had been you could only see a few centimetres in front of your nose. It wasn't just the steam, there was no sun. The sky was dead grey, as if it had eaten all that was left of the light and made itself sick. I felt sick too. Sick as shit.

'Hang on a mo!' Duke said suddenly. He turned to the other three and muttered something I couldn't hear.

'You're pulling my tit,' I heard one of them say.

'Fuckin' oath!' was Rooster's reaction.

'What's your other name, boy?' Duke asked, spinning round to eyeball me again.

I tried to outstare him, the way we did at school as a game, but my eyes kept sliding down from his face to his hands, on the backs of which the word PATU was tattooed. 'N . . . Nene,' I stuttered.

'Max Nene.'

'Can I go now?'

'You hear that bros? He wants to push off. Haven't found your money have you?'

'Doesn't matter. Wasn't much.'

'Where you gunna push off to? The Boy's Home?'

I opened my mouth but the only sound that came out was a faint snap from the back of my throat.

'You could come with us,' Duke said. He sounded that casual you'd think he was talking about the weather.

'Can't,' I said, my voice squeaking like a rusty door. 'Gotta . . .'

'Gotta what?'

'Can't,' I repeated.

Duke bent down so his face was close to mine. His breath smelt worse than the rotten eggs. 'You know what a prospect is, boy?' he asked.

I shook my head. I didn't think there was any piss left in me but there was. A fresh stream of it was scalding my left leg. Why didn't they just throw me in the porridge and be done with it?

'He's only a kid,' the one who looked the most Maori said.

'A kid with enterprise,' Duke pointed out. 'Aren't I always telling you we can use enterprise?'

'Yeah but . . .'

'Somethin' bothering you, Cutter? Reckon he's too young to be a prospect?'

'Somethin' like that.'

'Yeah . . . Well . . .' Duke stretched the words out like they were chewing gum. 'Good to know you've got the boy's interests at heart.'

The next thing I knew Duke was smiling right at me. It didn't stop me feeling scared but it probably stopped me shitting myself. With a glance over his shoulder at Cutter he told me things were going to be choice for me from now on. I was to go with Cutter, who'd take care of me. He, Duke, would see me later. I definitely felt better then. I'd already sussed that Cutter was on my side.

'OK man, you cut tracks now,' Duke said to Cutter. 'You too, kid,' he added.

And that was how it happened. How I joined the gang. Not that I was anything more than a dogsbody for the first few years. A prospect, they called me. Only I wasn't like the other prospects, who'd asked to join. I'd been invited. Not that I didn't have to earn my place when the time came — you don't get to be a patched member by running messages and delivering bags of dope. You have to perform — deal the dirt in the way they tell you. But I was a fast

86

learner. I knew the score. The sooner I was patched up the better for me. 'Once you're a patched member you're marked for life,' Cutter told me.

But that was what I wanted. To wear the mark of belonging for the rest of my life.

Those four blokes, Duke, Rooster, Cutter and Mick, they were the heart of the gang. They lived in this neat house by the lake. That was where Cutter took me that day, and that was where I lived from then on, apart from the times I was inside.

I really liked that house. You couldn't see it from the road. It had this huge corrugated iron fence all the way round it. But once you were through the gates it was like a real family home. It reminded me of my Nan's. Not that the women who lived there were anything like Nan. Raewyn, she was Duke's woman; she was a real tough cookie. You didn't mess with her if you knew what was good for you. Then there was Marama, whose brother Hemi was part of the gang, though he didn't live with us. Marama was OK so long as she didn't get into the dope. When she did all hell broke loose. I remember this one night she decided to have a go at Raewyn. Big mistake! Marama ended up in hospital.

There were various other women who came and went, when there were rages and that, but the only other resident was Trudi. Trudi was blonde and sexy though she didn't take care of herself so she sometimes looked pretty crook. She was a good sort though. She'd give it to anyone in the gang who asked. I'd only been in the house three days when she came on to me. I knew I was OK then. Trudi would never come on to an outsider.

One of the first jobs I was given was looking after the dogs. There were four of them, evil-looking monsters with names to match. But actually they were sweet as butter once they got to know you. My favourite was the one called Satan, who used to sleep on the end of my bunk. The day he got old, and Rooster took him out and shot him, I hid in the shed by the lake, the same shed I hid in when I ran away from the Boys' Home, and howled as if I was a bloody dog myself.

Three years I looked after them pit bulls. I couldn't do much with them for the first couple months, not with everyone looking for me, but once that had stopped, and I'd grown a weasly moustache, the dogs and I could go anywhere. I liked that a lot. Being with them dogs made me feel invincible.

It was just after my fifteenth birthday that Duke announced someone else — a spotty-faced prospect called Shane — would be looking after the dogs from now on. I was needed for other things. I was that hacked off I nearly did a runner. Which would have landed me in the shit and no mistake. We were a disciplined organisation. Duke was the President and you didn't mess with him. I may not have been patched then, but I soon would be. Patched members never run away, not if they know what's good for them.

The name of our gang was The Patus. That's what you got tattooed on your hands when you became a patched member. Patu means weapon, so that's what we were, human weapons. 'Any particular sort of weapon?' I asked Duke on my second day.

'The sort I can rely on,' he answered.

13

At the end of that long afternoon with Greg, light-headed from the wine I'd drunk with Tess, I came back to my flat, collapsed on the bed and slept for twelve hours. In the morning I phoned Queenie, but the line was engaged. I kept trying throughout the day with the same result.

Next day, in the wake of the visit to Ani, I try the line again. Frustrated, I phone Telecom to see if there's a fault. 'Line checks out fine,' I'm told. 'If it goes on being busy we can interrupt for you.' I wonder what the operator, whose excessive friendliness irritates me, would say if she knew the call I was trying to make was in response to instructions from a dead man.

That night I fall into the strange territory between sleeping and waking where, according to one theory, ideas are hatched and connections made. I don't know if that's what's happening to me. All I know is, I can't escape into sleep and I can't wake myself up.

Cecil and I are walking in Regent's Park. It's the spring of 1984. We have been together seven years. All around us are the signs of new life: daffodils and crocuses making pools of colour on the grass; ducks leading their flotillas of babies on the Serpentine; trees struggling into leaf. Our mood is anything but spring-like.

'Why won't you come?' I demand, for the third or fourth time. 'If you loved me . . .'

'Renate, that's not fair,' Cecil interjects. 'This has got nothing to do with whether I love you or not. You know how things are with my mother. I can't leave her . . .'

'She's suffering from depression, Cecil. Not terminal cancer.'

'Besides, I don't have the money.'

'That's because you keep lending . . .'

'Don't start. I don't tell you how to spend *your* money.'

'Maybe you should. Maybe if you cared what I did with my money . . .'

Unexpectedly, Cecil grins. 'If you're going to tell me that's all it takes to get you to marry me,' he says. 'Really Renate, you are the most perverse . . .'

'No one gets married any more,' I protest, defensively.

'So you keep telling me.'

I give a fierce kick to a piece of turf. What we are quarrelling about is my wish to return to New Zealand. Not forever, I'm not asking that, but for a year maybe, or two. The country's crying out for doctors, I've told Cecil. I don't actually know that, but it seems like a reasonable assumption. But I've made no secret of my real reason for wanting to go back after an absence of nearly a decade. I want to see my family, and I want to see the friends of my youth, Tessa Mayhew in particular. Her regular letters have acted as an antidote to the seductive distractions of life in London. With every letter she has reminded me who I am and where I come from. But Cecil is being as obstinate as the piece of turf I've been trying to dislodge from its roots. 'Look,' I say, trying a new tack, 'I know you think there are no real differences between us, culturally. That the last two decades have done away with such barriers, but you're wrong. There are no Maori in England for a start. How on earth are you supposed to understand me . . .'

'Maybe if we lived together we'd start to understand each other . . . We don't have to be married, Renate. Just live as if we were.'

I look up at the man I love so passionately and feel a sudden urge to punch him. He's right of course. We should live together. I'm not even sure why I keep saying no. Partly, I think, because I'm afraid. Things are so perfect as they are. Why risk changing them?

But of course things aren't perfect. We wouldn't be quarrelling if they were.

'Cecil Langton, I hate you sometimes,' I mutter.

'I know.'

'Don't you ever hate me?'

'Well at this precise moment I'm not very keen on you. Especially as you've chosen to have this fight in the park, with half the population of London as witnesses.'

'I haven't seen you for nearly a week'

'And whose fault is that?'

I swallow back my protest. Usually it's Cecil who can't get away. An elderly patient to visit; a child in hospital; a young man with suicidal tendencies. 'You make yourself available to every Tom, Dick and Harry,' I have complained bitterly in the past. 'How about making yourself available to me?' But this week the pressure of work has been mine. Last-minute rewrites of a television play. With the studio lined up and the actors cast, it was work that couldn't be put off. 'All I ever get is the exhausted bit of you,' I complain. 'I want the man you are in Cornwall.'

'You have your deadlines,' Cecil replies calmly. 'I have my Hippocratic oath.'

'I thought doctors didn't take that any more.'

'You know what I mean.'

We walk on through the silky air, the words of accusation lying heavy between us. When Cecil stops and pulls me into his arms, I resist at first. But then he says, whispering in my ear, 'You go to New Zealand, darling. It's time you saw your family. I'll still be here when you get back.'

'And if I don't come back?'

'Then I'll have to come over and kidnap you.'

The kiss we exchange is long and tender. I don't care that we are attracting attention. Cecil's partner, Robert, has told me we attract attention anyway, with Cecil being so tall and bony, and me what he cheerfully refers to as a pipsqueak.

When the kiss is over, Cecil glances at his watch — a gesture I hate — and we turn back towards the gates. Our time together is over.

I didn't go back to New Zealand, not till I met Greg. When it came down to it I couldn't bring myself to leave Cecil. A year later he was dead. Is that why the thought of spring always fills me with sadness?

Three weeks pass. I reply to letters, send off faxes and deal with the pile of work marked 'Urgent'. Every few days I phone Maggie to enquire after Greg. She promises to let me know if there is any change. I answer the phone when it rings, but leave the recorded messages till the end of the month. The relief when I finally play the tape and there is no message from Max is so great I burst into tears.

When the fit of weeping stops I blow my nose, then try to take stock of what's been happening to me. For a start, who have I been crying for? Max? Greg? Cecil? Myself?

I think about Queenie, and try her number again. What I should do, of course, is drive over there. Queenie wouldn't expect advance warning. But something — the fear of what she has to tell me perhaps — holds me back.

'You're suffering from an overactive imagination,' my mother would say if she knew what I was thinking. 'What you need is a long, healthy walk.'

My mother lives in Hamilton; near enough to drive there and back in a day. I love her very much, but somehow I can't picture myself telling her about Max's ghostly appearances. Greg now, I could tell her about him. In fact I *should* tell her. His accident would have been reported in the papers. It can only be a matter of time before someone mentions it to her.

My mother never liked Greg. I see that as a mark in her favour now. She's a bit of a snob, my mother; predisposed to like QCs. But she never took to Greg. 'But why do you have to marry him?' she said, when I dropped that particular bombshell.

'After all, you never married Cecil.'

I didn't like to tell her the real reason: that I thought it would make us safe; that I'd come to believe there was some magic in marriage that meant I wouldn't lose him, as I'd lost Cecil.

'Mum? Hi! How are you? Is this a bad time?'

'Darling! How lovely . . . Is something wrong?'

'Why do you say that?'

'You sound as if you've got a cold.'

'Hay fever. You know how it is. Unhealthy place, Auckland.'

'Something *is* wrong, isn't it?

Is this the moment to tell her about Max? As far as Mum is concerned Max was a young friend of mine, an *unfortunate* young friend, (Mum's fond of words like *unfortunate*) who was killed in a car accident. Probably, though she'd never say so to my face, she thinks his death was a 'blessed release'. 'So sad for his mother,' she said, when I told her. 'But then perhaps he's been saved from an even worse fate. The papers did say . . .'

'You don't believe that garbage, do you?'

'You're upset, darling. It's only natural. After all you did for him . . .'

No, I don't think I'll tell Mum about Max.

'It's Greg,' I say into the phone. 'He's had an accident. I thought you might have read about it. It's serious. He's in a coma.'

'I've been busy,' my mother responds. She sounds peevish. Surely she doesn't think I'm accusing her? 'I haven't looked at a paper for days.'

'It's all right, Mum. It doesn't matter. I just thought you should know.'

'Well of course . . .'

'Maggie phoned me,' I tell her.

'An accident. You mean in a car?'

'He fell asleep at the wheel.'

'He was always a terrible driver.'

I smile into the phone. At least she didn't make a crack about his drinking.

'Odd that Maggie . . .'

'The doctors are hopeful. He should . . . I don't envy Maggie, Mum. Greg is an impossible patient.'

'A woman who steals a man from under his wife's nose, well, I don't have polite words. But you're right, it can't be easy. Nor for you, darling. I know you still have feelings . . .'

'I went to see him. He looks awful. His face is all smashed up . . .'

'Do you want me to come up? I can easily put things off here. In fact why don't I do that? I could drive up first thing tomorrow.'

'There's no need, Mum. Honest. I might come and see you though. Be good to get out of Auckland. Would Sunday be OK?'

'I'm on duty at church, but I'll be free by lunchtime. Can you stay? I'd really like it if you'd stay.'

The fact that my eyes start to prick has nothing to do with Greg or Max or my bottled-up grief. It's my mother's invitation that has brought on this fit of self-pity. My mother's been a widow for so many years now she's made an art form of living on her own. My brother and I call her 'The Busy Widow'. We invite her to come and see us (my brother is a builder in Palmerston North), but she almost always refuses. Too many charities to manage; too much church work. In all the years I lived in England I never once persuaded her to come to Europe, despite the fact she had a German grandmother, after whom I am named. It wasn't that she couldn't afford it. Dad had left her well provided for.

'Thanks, Mum,' I say into the phone. 'I might just do that.'

Feeling better than I have in days I step out on to the balcony of my flat, and let the perverse beauty of Auckland play on my senses. For once the haze that usually surrounds the distant view is absent, and I can see the harbour. By night, it's the flashing lights of the casino tower that draw my eye. I hated that tower when it went up. I hated the thought that the city's skyline would be dominated by such a profane object. If I'd known then that Max was a regular player, I'd have hated it even more.

'It was Mum who started it,' Pete told me at the tangi. 'She and Ela won $700 the week the casino opened. Once Max got wind of that he was a goner.'

I should have questioned Pete, not let my astonishment — surely if Max had got the gambling bug I'd have known about it — silence me. One thing I do know about Max is that he never did anything by halves. If he gambled, it would have been for high stakes. And if he lost, there would have been debts — debts which could well be linked to his death.

I *will* question Pete, I decide, turning my eyes from the harbour to the despised but, by day, curiously innocuous tower. And if *he* can't shed any light, I'll have a go at Queenie. Even if it means turning up unannounced.

I take in a deep, scented breath. The hedge surrounding these apartments is tangled with jasmine. It's sweet, late-afternoon smell fills me with melancholy. Greg's garden, so called, was swathed in jasmine. Where there had once been native bush there are now banks covered with wandering jew, stands of ginger and clumps of cutty grass, all of which resist the most herculean efforts to remove them. When I pointed out to Greg the damage being done to his home by the encroaching creepers, some of which had found their way around windows and doors, he just laughed. 'This place will outlive us both,' he boasted.

Feeling unaccountably chilled, I move back into the living room. The sky behind me is the colour of Greg's eyes. Is that why I can't bear to look at it any more?

Well Max, I think, if you're going to haunt me, now's your moment. It's been three weeks since he materialised at the hospital. Three weeks without a murmur from him; or from Cecil, who has retreated even from my waking dreams. I should be relieved. But what I'm feeling is neglected.

Max told me once he believed he would always be protected by his kaitiaki, his spiritual guardians. When I asked him to explain, he said they were like angels, only since they were drawn from the ranks of his ancestors, the relationship was more personal. 'I mean, when I think of poor Mary being scared witless by the Angel Gabriel, because she didn't know who the fuck he was, I reckon it's better to be Maori. At least we know who's haunting us. And they're not messengers, they're protectors.'

'Is that what you are, Max?' I ask, hoping to conjure him up with my words. 'And in case you're wondering, I have every intention of going to see Queenie. I'm just waiting for the right moment.'

I wait, counting the seconds as they pass; but the only thing that moves is one of the curtains, touched by the breeze from the balcony.

When I lived with Greg I left the curtains open all night. The one true thing he told me about his home was that it was completely private. Being free to move about the house half-dressed or naked is one of the things I miss about my life back then. But I don't miss the house, nor the days spent trying to turn a wilderness into a garden. 'Waste of time,' Greg would grumble, if I asked for his help. 'It's the view that will sell this place, not the garden.' But he was never going to sell, was he? Those were just words, to trap me.

'No,' I say, out loud. 'I refuse to be haunted by you, Greg, or by your house. That life is over.'

'What happened to Cressida's mother?' I asked Greg, the day I finally agreed to live with him. He had just made me a solemn promise. If I would get the house cleaned up and the visible rubbish removed from the garden, he would sell. He'd do the work himself, only he had so little time. Buoyed by the thought of the future, we'd opened a bottle of wine and fallen happily into bed. Now it was early evening. We were sitting on the front verandah, the one overlooking the Waitemata. A lone tui serenaded us from a surviving kowhai tree. When Greg asked me what I thought of the view and the scented, song-filled evening, I didn't hesitate. 'It's beautiful,' I acknowledged.

'Nothing happened to her,' Greg said, in answer to my question. 'She left. End of story.'

'Yes, but why? You'd been married for more than ten years. Why so suddenly . . .'

'There was nothing sudden about it, Renate.'

'Did you just fall out of love, was that it?'

I should have stopped there. I should have heeded the warning signs. But I went on with what Greg subsequently called my 'obsessive cross-examination' (a phrase he used repeatedly, until I learned to leave the subject of his failed marriages alone). And so a day that had begun in lyrical hopefulness ended in another gloomy silence and I was left none the wiser about my predecessor.

A week after that failed conversation, Cressida came to live with us. She was eleven years old. Her mother, Molly, was a potter and wanted space to get on with her work. Greg, whose two other children, both boys, were by that time leading independent lives, made no apology for the fact that I now had to take on the duties of a mother. 'You can write when Cress is at school,' he said. 'So long as you're here when she gets home.'

It wasn't an auspicious start, but Cressida and I soon learned to tolerate one another. Genuine affection was longer in coming, but when it did the strength of the bond surprised me. Cressida was — is — spunky, clever and chillingly unsentimental. When she announced, at the age of fourteen, that she was going back to live with her mother there was nothing Greg or I could do to dissuade her. Four years later she turned her back on all of us and took off for England. But by then I was in the middle of a drama of my own.

The day Greg decided he no longer wanted me in his life he piled my possessions on the side verandah, changed the locks on the doors and took off in his car. I'd gone to a concert in the Domain with Max and some of the younger members of his family. I'd urged Greg, who'd only just been told about Cressida's departure, to come with me. At the very least I thought it might distract him. The concert was to include a kapahaka group trained and led by Max. My hope was that if Greg saw what Max could do, how creative he could be, his antagonism might lessen a little. But mostly I just wanted to distance Greg from his anger with Molly, whom he blamed for Cressida's flight. Molly was a bad mother — a middle-aged woman who persisted in behaving like a hippie. Cressida would never have turned her back on a university education if her mother hadn't encouraged her. 'Off you go, darling,' were the words Greg attributed to her. 'You don't need university. Life will be your teacher.' If anything happened to his daughter, Greg muttered darkly, he'd know who to blame.

I didn't tell Greg Max was involved in the concert. I'd learned from bitter experience to leave Max's name out of our conversations. Instead I used Greg's love of open-air concerts and the music of the Pacific to urge him to accompany me. But he was having none of it. And when I got back from that long, happy afternoon, all that was left of my marriage was a trail of scattered belongings on the verandah.

What followed seems so incredible now I have difficulty putting it into words. It wasn't just the locks Greg had changed, it was his phone number as well. Every effort to contact him ended in failure. If I tried to call him at the office I was told he was not available. And I was too proud to call his sons. All I could do was wait outside the house, certain he must return eventually. Five nights I spent shivering in the bush before sanity, in the shape of Tess, reasserted itself. The next day, urged on by Tess, I marched into Greg's office and demanded to speak to him. That was when I learned about Maggie. 'We're living together,' he told me. 'She understands about loyalty, even if you don't.'

Perhaps I don't want Greg to get better at all. Perhaps I think he deserved this accident.

14

The day after my phone call to my mother, I load my car up with fresh food from the supermarket and drive to South Auckland. Had Max not died this might have been my first visit to Queenie's house. I used to think Max didn't want me to get close to his family — something to do, I figured, with that sense of shame he talked about — but now I don't think it was that at all. If I've learned anything about Max in the weeks since he died, it's that he kept the various parts of his life, including his passion for gambling, tightly compartmentalised. Despite what he wrote for me, often under duress, it wasn't his past he wanted to bring to our relationship, but his future. The role he'd assigned me was that of guide and mentor. The trouble was, he neglected to explain just what kind of a future he was planning.

As I speed down the southern motorway I reflect that of all the unanswered questions I have about Max, probably the most unanswerable is, 'what did you want, Max? What did you want to do with your life?' For all I know he could have been planning the revolution with Ani.

I park my car on the side of the road, aware I'm being watched from behind at least four sets of twitching curtains. From the outside Queenie's house looks like all the others in the street. Built of wood, badly in need of a paint, it was originally a State house, but is now, under the new user-pays regime, run by a Housing Corporation which charges market rents. Queenie pays $260 a week for a house with a leaking roof, mildewed walls and faulty wiring.

How many people live with Queenie is not a question that could ever be answered accurately. Some nights it's just her and her husband, Will Walsh, the resident grandchild and Vincent and his wife, Gloria, who are waiting for their names to come up on a housing list. Other nights the numbers could swell by as many as ten. During the tangi there were at least twenty of us sleeping wherever we could find a mattress. The night before the burial the number rose to nearer forty. But no one sleeps the night before a burial.

As I walk up the broken path to Queenie's front door I wonder why Max chose to live with Pete, not Queenie, when he came out of prison. From what I've seen of Will, he wouldn't have posed a problem. His easy-going nature was much in evidence over the days of the tangi. Was Queenie hurt by her son's decision I wonder? She doesn't mince words when it comes to talking about Ani's *defection*.

Naturally I wondered about Max's decision at the time. I had the feeling he'd hoped I might ask him to live with Greg and me, but of course that was out of the question. I hadn't met Queenie then, but whenever the subject of Max's release came up, I'd assumed that was where he would go. Now that I know the kind of open house Queenie runs — daughters, cousins, nieces, sons all regularly seek refuge with her — I find it even more puzzling that Max chose to move in with his youngest brother. 'Closer to town,' was the explanation he gave me at the time. 'Closer to the action.' The grin on his face should have alerted me.

I stop at the porch and remove my shoes. Judging by the footwear already discarded there, the whanau is present in some numbers. I notice a pair of elegant, high-heeled boots amongst a heap of childrens' shoes and wonder if Ani is paying one of her rare visits. I get my answer when Gloria comes to greet me. Gloria, a Pakeha, is one of the few members of Queenie's extended family with a regular job. She works in a dress shop in downtown Auckland. Something about her way of dressing reminds me of Maggie. But I don't let that affect me as we greet each other with a hug. 'I'm pregnant, can you tell?' she whispers in my ear. 'Haven't told Queenie yet.'

'Why not? She'll be thrilled.'

'*She* will be. I'm not.'

Bunched at the back of Gloria are three small children, and an older girl I recognise as Ela's eldest, Bethany. Close behind them come Queenie's two Rottweiler dogs, ugly-looking specimens answering to the unlikely names of Holly and Molly. I say hi to the children and pat the dogs gingerly. Even keeping my distance I can smell their foul breath.

I walk into the living room, wave to the assembled company and move towards Queenie. She's sitting in her usual chair, Ela's youngest on her knee, a cigarette in her mouth. 'Wondered when you'd come,' she says, as I stoop to embrace her.

'You're a difficult woman to get hold of, Queenie,' I retaliate. 'I've lost count of the number of times I've tried to phone you.'

She grins and waves her hand at the only spare seat in the room, a space on the sofa between Gloria and Ela.

I smile at Ela's baby. Ela's husband (from whom she is currently estranged) is of Dalmatian origin, but Ela's combination of Maori and Samoan features has been passed on to her son. The boy stares back at me impassively.

'That'll be Walter,' Queenie says, shaking her head in mock annoyance. 'Phone's never out of his hand. Don't ask me what he gets up to, but I'll lay a bet it isn't legal.'

'It's not always Walter,' Ela protests. 'Lily was on the phone last night for an hour and a half.'

'And you couldn't speak to your fancy man, I know.' Queenie gives an exaggerated sigh. 'Just as well, if you ask me.'

'How are things, Renate?' The question is asked by Lily, Queenie's youngest daughter. She smiles at me from behind the backs of the two children squashed into an armchair with her. Until the tangi I didn't really know Lily, though I felt as if I did. She and her brother Pete, the offspring of Queenie's marriage to Will, are by far the most easy-going of Max's siblings.

Knowing her better, as I do now, has only increased my liking for her. As for Max — who never made any secret of his preference for female company — Lily's four small children probably had something to do with him choosing to live with Pete. Pete was, and still is, unencumbered. 'Are you OK?' Lily persists.

The last thing I want to do in this crowded, smoke-filled room is talk about myself, but with Lily's kind eyes fixed on me I can't seem to manufacture a suitable response. 'I cry a lot,' I admit.

'We all do that,' Lily comforts.

'Nothin' wrong with cryin',' Vincent remarks.

I tell myself not to be sentimental. The lump in my throat is a natural response to this family's emotional permissiveness. Was it Max's fault or the family's that a distance was kept? If Max had seen more of them would he still be alive today? What was he doing in that car? Was he just joyriding? Or was something more sinister going on?

'I don't like it,' Queenie announces, into the gap that's opened up in the conversation. 'Somethin' should have been done by now.'

'Now, Mum!' a male voice cautions. It's not Vincent, but Walter, entering the room with a crate of beer. He drops it on the floor, kisses his mother, hefts a chair in from the kitchen and plonks himself down. I feel myself beginning to sweat. Six adults and assorted children in a small, overheated room is not a recipe for comfort. I wonder if I'm becoming claustrophobic. It can happen as you get older. It's not just the living people I feel pressing in on me, it's the photos covering the wall; particularly, in pride of place above the television, a large, very flattering photo of Max. Judging by the long hair, it was taken at the same time as the one he gave me. I've been trying not to stare at it ever since I came into the room.

While Queenie and Walter bandy words, I glance at the television (which is on, but mercifully with the sound turned down), and wonder if I can ask someone to open a window. Apart from the children and Lily, I'm the only one not smoking.

Hanging on the wall behind Walter is a large painting on velvet of a wharekura. Max's tribal affiliations were complex — Ngapuhi from his father, Ngati Maniapoto from his mother, kinship connections with both Ngati Tuwharetoa and Tuhoe — but when I asked on whose marae the meeting house stood, no one seemed to know.

I watch Walter patiently explaining things to his mother, and think what a formidable warrior he would have made. Like Max. He's a bigger man than his older brother, with a puku hanging over his belt betraying his liking for beer; but he resembles Max: same fine skin (lightly tattooed in Walter's case); same wide, flat nose; same warm brown eyes. Walter is married, with five children, one of whom lives permanently with Queenie. According to Ani, Walter spends most of his time at his mother's to be near his son. So like Lily (whose husband, a long-distance truck driver, is often away overnight), he's part of the floating population of the house.

'But what the papers said was wrong,' Queenie insists, for the third time. 'You know that as well as I do, Walter. Somethin' has to be done.'

I wait for Walter's quiet rebuff; but this time what he says is, 'I keep tellin' you, Mum. We can't do nuthin' till we have the coroner's report.'

Of course, I think, looking at Walter with grateful surprise, you're right. I'd forgotten all about the coroner. He will have answers; if not about Max's life, then at least about his death. He may even solve the puzzle, if there is one, of Max's connection with the casino.

'And you think coroners tell the truth?' Queenie challenges bitterly.

Walter scratches the soles of his feet. The dogs look up from their somnambulant positions and wriggle their noses. 'The coroner's not the same as the police, Mum,' he explains. 'If Max was . . .' Walter glances at me. Why do I get the feeling the frown on his face is meant as a warning?

'Was what?' I prompt.

'Murdered,' Walter says.

Murdered! The word jams at the back of my throat. I feel as if someone has forced me to swallow a live coal. 'Murdered,' I say hoarsely. 'There was nothing in the papers about . . .'

'It's just Mum's theory,' Walter mutters.

'But why . . . How? Is it something to do with the Patus? Please tell me,' I urge, glancing from one pair of averted eyes to another. 'You must know something, otherwise . . .' I stop, struck by the silence in the room. 'You believe it, don't you?' I accuse. 'All of you. You think . . .'

'We don't know what to believe,' Lily interjects quietly.

'It's only a theory,' Walter repeats. 'Possible, but not probable,' he says, looking straight at his mother.

Gloria, next to me, crushes her cigarette in a saucer and lights another. I close my eyes just for a second, but in that time I see Greg. The smile on his face tells me exactly what he's thinking. 'This isn't some war orphan you're dealing with, Renate, some innocent victim of circumstances. This is a convicted murderer.'

'They shouldn't be allowed to print lies like that,' Queenie says, in answer to Walter. 'I know my Max. He's done some bad things in his life, but he wasn't like they said.'

I think back to the day after the accident, to those unforgettable headlines: *Man killed after high-speed chase. Gang member killed in freak accident*. I should have read what followed more carefully. I shouldn't have let my cowardice inhibit me. At the time I told myself I didn't need to do more than skim read. I know this country. I know what kind of press we have. A man like Max — Maori, an ex-gang-member (strange how that 'ex' was left out of the headline) — is never allowed to forget his crimes.

'So when do we get to see this coroner's thingy?' Ela asks, her voice, like her expression, sulky. 'Why's it taking so long?'

'Because they're hidin' somethin',' Queenie answers.

'Give it a rest, Mum,' Walter pleads.

'Don't you use that tone with me, boy. You may be the eldest of my sons now, but that doesn't give you the right to tell me what to do.'

While Walter seeks distraction in his itchy feet, Queenie reminds us, as if we needed reminding, that the police treated the scene of Max's accident as a crime scene. 'Why would they do that if they weren't on to somethin'?' she says.

'Well of course they were on to somethin',' Ela pouts. 'They were chasin' him, weren't they?'

'That's because the car was stolen,' I remind her.

'Wasn't the car they were after,' Queenie declares, thrusting her mokoed chin at her daughter in a gesture of defiance. 'It was the driver.'

'So the car wasn't stolen?'

'I didn't say that.'

Ela turns to the television. Her eyes glaze over. 'So what was Max doin' then?' she asks.

'That's what we have to find out,' Queenie says.

One of the children, bored by the long faces and solemn talk of the adults, turns the television up. I make a move to turn it down, but Ela stops me. 'Lotto results,' she explains. 'Never know ya luck,' she adds, winking at me in a momentary display of animation.

'Does anyone know who this other man was?' I ask, looking round the room. I still haven't come to terms with *murdered*.

While I wait for someone to answer, I go over what I know. The driver of the car escaped without injury. Escaped, period. So far as I know the police still haven't found him.

'Pete reckons he might know,' Vincent eventually answers.

I look with interest at the usually silent Vincent. He must be in his twenties still, but he looks a decade older. Short, heavily built, with thinning brown hair, I can't help wondering if he resembles his father, the mysterious Samoan no one wants to talk about. The other son of that union, Ela's twin, Paea, has a job in the freezing works at Horotiu. He was pointed out to me at the tangi but I never got to talk to him. In fact he didn't seem to talk to anyone very much. Each time I caught sight of him he was on his own.

'He found a diary,' Vincent explains.

'What sort of a diary?'

'You know, those things business people have. Whadda ya call them?'

'Filofax,' Ela says, through a yawn.

'Max had a Filofax?' I ask incredulously.

It's Lily who answers me. 'He had a mobile phone too, he was gunna use it to go into business. I was s'posed to keep quiet about it, but I reckon now . . .'

I shake my head in disbelief. Not that I think Lily is lying. Max was fond of his youngest sister. It doesn't surprise me that he should have confided in her. What does surprise, and hurt, is that he didn't also confide in *me*.

At the time he died Max had been out of work for four months. In the last conversation we had about employment he told me, and I believed him, that he was in line for a job teaching kapahaka in schools. That, with the carving he was planning to do, and the bits and pieces of writing I could still wring out of him, suggested he had a bright, creative future ahead of him. Now I'm asked to believe that what he was really up to during those months of idleness was some kind of *business*. A business that may, if Queenie's theory is right, have got him murdered.

'So what's in this Filofax?' I ask Vincent. 'Have you seen it?'

Vincent shakes his head. 'All Pete told me was that Max was meetin' someone the day he died. Roy someone . . .'

'That would be Roy Harawira,' a voice announces from the doorway.

I turn to see Queenie's husband, Will, laden down with plastic bags, resting against the doorpost. Will was a postman before his legs gave out on him, but he still has the healthy complexion of a man who works out of doors. These days Will spends most of his time fishing. 'Kai,' he says, pointing at the bags. 'Come on, kids.' He jabs a finger in the direction of the heap of children sprawled in front of the television. 'Mussels,' he explains to me, though I've already figured that out from the smell. 'Kids know what to do.'

His arrival is the signal for Walter to start opening the beer. I want to ask Will what he knows about Roy Harawira but there are too many other things going on. I learned during the tangi that it's better to stay quiet during these times of intense activity. Will, who has lowered himself onto a cushion within sight of the kitchen, supervises the cooking of the mussels with quiet authority. It was Will who saw that everyone was fed during the tangi. No mean task with so many people coming through the house. While Will toiled over a huge cooker set up for the occasion in a neighbour's shed, Queenie, regal in the same red and green shawl she is wearing today, stayed in this room, surrounded by mourners. Her place was next to her son's open coffin.

I turn my back on the kitchen, determined not to let my aversion to mussels drive me out of the room. 'Roy Harawira?' I prompt, when there's a lull in the activity. 'Do you know him, Will?'

'Everyone knows Harawira,' Will answers.

'Who is he?'

Will looks over at Queenie. I can't interpret the message that passes between them, but whatever it is it allows him to answer my question. 'Roy Harawira is a drug dealer,' he tells me.

I fix my eyes on Queenie. If everyone but me knows who Harawira is, then Queenie knows too, but whether she knew he was the man in the car with Max is something I'll have to wait to find out.

Since nobody else seems to want to follow up on this revelation, I take the plunge myself, and ask Vincent if the police have been told about Roy Harawira. But it's not Vincent who answers me, it's Queenie. 'No point talking to them,' she says.

'But if what you say is true, that it's the driver they're looking for, then surely . . .'

'You think they'd take back what they said about Max? You think they'd print an apology?'

'That was the press, not the police.'

'Same thing.'

I take in a breath, and hold it as long as I can. The smell of boiling mussels has now totally overpowered the smell of cigarette smoke. I murmur my excuses, and walk out of the room.

Opening the front door, I take in a huge gulp of fresh air, make a space for myself amongst the shoes and sit down. The words, 'Max was back on drugs. Max was murdered', are repeating themselves in my mind, like a mantra. 'Me and drugs is bad news,' Max said, on one of my visits to Pare. 'Me and alcohol as well, come to that. I'd never have got into this mess if it weren't for them.' On another occasion he announced his intention of campaigning against drugs and alcohol when he got out of prison. 'You could find out about it for me, Renate,' he suggested, flashing me one of his irresistible grins. 'Programmes in schools. Stuff like that. Maybe I could train as one of them counsellors.'

'So this is where you got to,' a voice says from behind me.

For a crazy moment I think it's Max come back to haunt me. But it's not, it's Will, smiling benignly down on me.

I move to make room for him. I've always felt easy with Will. I've wondered sometimes if it's because we're both Pakeha, but actually I think it has more to do with Will's unflappable nature. I've no idea how old he is. He has one of those craggy faces that seem, like mountains, to be ageless.

'You bring that kai in the kitchen?' he asks.

'Just a bit of fruit and veg.'

'And the rest.'

'How are the mussels doing?'

'Fattest I've seen this year. Found this bed no one else seems to know about.'

'Is Queenie all right, Will? She seems . . .'

'Early days, Renate, early days. Eldest son and all that. Hard to let go.'

'But they weren't, you know . . .'

'Close?'

'Yeah.'

'They are now.'

I nod, though I'm not sure I understand him. Is he saying that Queenie loves Max more in death than she did in life? That would be terrible if it were true. Max, unlike his siblings, never called his mother 'Mum'. She was always Queenie.

While I pick away at the strands of Max's life, Will picks at the moss on the porch with his knife. The metallic scrape of the blade grates on my nerves. To distract myself I begin to arrange the discarded shoes into pairs. That sets me thinking about socks, and how Cecil used to complain the washing machine ate his socks because he only ever seemed to have odd ones.

'Do *you* think Max was murdered?' I ask, when I can do no more with the shoes.

The scraping sound continues for a few more moments, then it stops. 'Don't know,' Will answers, 'and that's the honest truth. But something's not right. Think about it for a moment. Max was dead by the time the police got there. And the driver had scarpered. What does that say to you?'

'Oh God, Will, don't ask me. I didn't even know till today that there was any question of . . . I knew he was in trouble, of course. Why else would the police have been chasing him? But I never thought, never imagined . . . It doesn't make sense. He'd been out of prison two years. Why would he suddenly . . .'

'Do you always see the best in people, Renate?'

'I see what's there.'

Will touches my hand. 'I think, where Max was concerned, you saw what he wanted you to see.'

I want to refute that, but I'm overwhelmed suddenly by a sense of futility. Does no one know the truth? Or are there several truths, and all I'm doing is stumbling about amongst them?

Tomorrow I'll be with my mother. The thought soothes. I won't be able to tell her about any of this, of course. I doubt that, even in the line of charity, she's ever encountered a family like this one. But it will be a relief to be back in her clean, well-ordered home.

'Did Queenie know it was Roy Harawira in that car?' I ask. 'That's if Vincent's theory's right, and it *was* him.'

'We'll know more when we have the coroner's report.'

It's not what I wanted to hear, but when Will resumes his scraping, I realise it's the only answer I'm going to get.

Max never expressed an opinion about Will Walsh. Which is odd, considering he's Lily and Pete's father. As I listen to the screech of blade on stone and watch the trail of ants Will's probing has unearthed, I wonder if Max's silence had anything to do with Will being a Pakeha. 'You should be worried, you know, Renate,' Max said to me once, grinning to show he was only half serious. 'Think about where you and your tribe are in the world, geographically speaking. Apart from Australia there isn't another Pakeha stronghold anywhere, not till you hit South America. And your Hawaiki is half a world away, a hell of a lot further than ours.'

'Can I give you some advice?' Will says, after we've sat for some moments without speaking.

'Fire away.'

'Queenie's a grand woman, no question, but she does get bees in her bonnet . . .'

I nod encouragingly. Max wanted me to visit his mother. He said she had things to tell me. What I haven't been able to work out, is whether my visit was supposed to help her or me.

Will folds his knife, and puts it back in his pocket. The ants have made a trail through the shoes. Soon they'll be heading down the steps and out on to the path. The thought of their journey exhausts me. 'She thinks you and Max, well . . .' Will gives me a rueful look. 'She reckons you should have got married,' he says.

'What?'

'A bee in her bonnet. I told you.'

'For heaven's sake, Will! Queenie knows how old I am. Same age as her, near enough. Wasn't she fifteen when she had him?'

'Fourteen.'

'The idea's preposterous!'

'She's persuaded herself Max would have settled down with you.'

'Rubbish! Sorry, Will, but that's complete and utter rubbish. Max and I loved each other, but not . . .'

'I agree. I just thought I should warn you, in case she brings it up.'

'Does she blame me for his death? Is that what you're trying to tell me?'

'Of course not.'

I count slowly to ten. I'm afraid if I open my mouth I'll say something I'll regret. Was this what you wanted me to hear, Max?

'It's not just Max's death,' Will goes on. 'It's the whole thing. The whole of his life. That stuff he was writing for you, he told me about it, I thought it sounded like just what he needed. Help to get him straight. Only thing was, he asked me not to tell Queenie about it. Actually got me to promise. He said it was between you and him, that he shouldn't even be telling me.'

I nod, hoping my expression won't betray what I'm thinking. That Max confided in Will has come as a shock, yet another reminder of my ignorance about him. Would Will be hurt if I told him Max hardly ever mentioned his name?

Will flattens his hands on his thighs and rubs vigorously. I'm not sure what the problem is with his legs, but I know he's often in pain. Queenie's lameness is the result of a childhood accident. 'Do you realise,' he says, raising his eyebrows at me, 'that you probably know more about him than his mother does?'

'There's a helluva lot I don't know,' I tell him.

'That's true for all of us.'

The thought that comes into my head then isn't easy to put into words. Especially with Max's ghost hovering at my shoulder. 'Are you telling me to stay away from Queenie?' I ask.

'No!' Will shakes his hands in front of him, as if shaking off excess water. 'Well, not exactly,' he qualifies. 'Look,' he goes on, 'I'm not sure I've got this right, but I think, what Queenie feels, is that you taught Max to want things he couldn't ultimately have. Not material things, not as such. More like skills, jobs. A life on your . . .' he grins at me, 'on *our* terms. Pakeha terms.'

'But he could have had those things. He could have had anything he wanted. He was very gifted.'

'No one's arguing with that.'

'Do you agree with Queenie? Do you think I . . .' The words stick in my throat. I'm consumed with the thought that this is

111

why Max wanted me to come. Which means he had those thoughts too. '. . . Messed things up,' I finish grimly.

This time Will doesn't just touch my hand, he takes hold of it. 'No, Renate,' he says. 'I don't. I think things were messed up for Max long before you came into his life. If you listen to Ani it goes back even further than that. A century and a half of being messed up.'

He makes a deprecating gesture, which I return. What is there to say in the face of such feelings? Will was quoting Ani, but he could just as easily have been speaking for Max. Ever since my visit to Ani I've been puzzling over her relationship with her elder brother. The impression she gave was that they weren't close, but I see now that they *were*, even if the connection existed more in Max's mind than his sister's. The synchronicity of their beliefs is too neat to be coincidence. No one else in Max's family uses political language, unless you count the regular grouching about the last government's batch of Maori MPs.

The question is, did Max and Ani share a common aim, one that Will and I, as Pakeha, could have no part in? Or was Max using Ani's words to write his own script?

'I don't want you and Queenie to fall out,' Will says, bringing my speculations to an end. 'I want you to think the best of her, just as you did of Max. Can you do that, Renate?'

I glance over my shoulder. If Max *is* with us I want him to hear my answer. 'Of course,' I say.

'Come on,' Will says, struggling to his feet. 'Your hands are like ice.'

15

I'm going to tell you how the world was made. There was Rangi, god of the sky, and Papa, the earth mother, and they were locked in an embrace so close their six sons lived in perpetual darkness. These sons were themselves gods. There was the god of the forest, and the god of the sea, and the god of the winds. There were the gods of wild foods and crops, and the god of mankind.

One day, Tane, the god of the forests, succeeded in parting Rangi from Papa. Suddenly, where there had been darkness there was light. But Rangi was heartbroken at being separated from his beloved. His tears fell as rain on the earth. Papa was heartbroken too. Her sorrow went up to Rangi in the form of rising mists.

Seeing this evidence of their parents' grief, the gods, their sons, felt sorry. They pinned stars onto Rangi's cloak, and clothed Papa in trees and ferns. But the rain and the mist continued.

Eventually, Tane, unable to appease his parents' sorrow, created a woman from the earth and mated with her. In this way the world as we know it began.

And as I see it it was a screwed-up bloody place from the start. I mean, how can anyone expect to be happy living in a universe created out of an act of violence? Tane murdered the happiness of his mother and father. Ask me, he should be in Pare, not me.

Personally I don't see much difference between what we did in the gang and what Tane did to Rangi and Papa. No, I take that back, I do see a difference. Half the time we brought people together, not separated them. And for those who were our friends there were favours, big favours. So we didn't murder happiness, we created it.

Those first few years, when I was in charge of the dogs, they were the best I reckon. No one ever said anything about school. Which didn't mean I didn't learn things. Raewyn taught me a lot of stuff, about a person's rights, stuff like that. It was Raewyn told me how to handle the pigs. All you had to do was give them your name, address and date of birth. That was the law. They could beat the shit out of you but you had your rights, same as the guys in suits. 'They're just another gang, kid,' she told me. 'Only difference is, there's more of them than us.'

Raewyn taught me how to knit too. You didn't know that about me, Renate, did you? That I'm an ace knitter. When I asked one of the screws if I could have knitting needles and wool in my cell he thought I was taking the piss. Like he thought a knitting needle was an offensive weapon! Reckon if they'd let me knit in this place, a lot of the shit that's happened wouldn't have been my shit. If you see what I mean.

I had to twist Raewyn's arm to get her to teach me. She thought I was having her on, told me to stuff off, act my age, crap like that. But when she saw I was serious she changed her tune. I cottoned on real quick too. Plain, pearl, cable, I could do the lot, no sweat. The bros gave me stick for a bit — reckoned I'd gone porangi, or worse — but they came round once they seen what I could do.

The first sweater I knitted was for Trudi. It was far out, even if I say so myself. It had this great rainbow across her tits which was what she wanted. When the others saw it they wasted no time putting in their orders. Duke, Cutter, Rooster, Mick, they all got jerseys made to their own specifications. Rooster wanted a great chook knitted on the front of his; Mick wanted a skull and crossbones; and Duke ordered a black jersey with a taiaha starting at the left shoulder and ending at the right hip.

I learned other things from Raewyn too, stuff about her life with Duke and how she dealt with it. She was a tough sheila, no one tougher, but that didn't stop Duke beating her up when he was off his face on dope. 'What you gotta understand, kid,' she said, 'is that all these gang guys, from the head honcho down, they're scared of

114

women. I know they spout all that stuff about a woman's place being in the bed and the kitchen and nowhere else but that's only 'cause they're scared.'

'Don't look scared,' I argued.

'Duke ever tell you the story of Hine-nui-te-po?' Raewyn asked me.

'Duke ain't Maori, is he?'

'Don't let him hear you say that.'

'You mean, he is Maori?'

'Knows more about Maoritanga than the rest of the bros put together.'

'Duke don't talk to me much.'

'That's 'cause you're a prospect. Lowest of the low.'

'Not for much longer.'

Raewyn gave me an odd look then, like there was this other person inside her who looked at things differently, even smiled differently. And talking of scared, I don't mind admitting I was more than a bit scared of her myself. It wasn't just her temper, which was awesome when roused. It wasn't just that she could have laid me out flat the way she did Marama that time. It was more to do with her mana. Raewyn had mana and no mistake. Even though she was a short-arse, which is what Duke called her, referring to her height. Short she may have been, and curvy rather than muscly, but she had a mouth on her that reminded me of my Auntie Petula. Come to think of it she was a lot like Auntie Petula, and not just 'cause she was short. She may not have known how to karanga, but I've seen her reduce a bunch of pigs stupid enough to knock on our door to silence. 'May I remind you, this is a family home,' she said. She spoke quietly, but that was always her way at the beginning. One look at her eyes and you knew she meant business. 'You don't have a warrant, do you? . . . Thought not. In that case, gentlemen, I suggest you take your aggression someplace else. There are plenty of other innocent citizens in this town for you to harass. You don't have to keep favouring us with your attentions.'

I've seen Rooster squirm under the force of Raewyn's tongue too, and that was when all she was doing was passing on a message from Duke. Rooster's a bit of a drongo, if you see what I mean. Not much upstairs. But even the others, Cutter and Mick, who're a bit more clued up, they didn't really know how to handle Raewyn. She was the Prez's woman, that was part of it. But I reckon it was more on account of her knowing things. And not being scared of nobody.

Which made the fact that she talked to me all the more sweet. Though it didn't last. Once I was patched up she treated me same as the others.

The only person who ever messed with Raewyn was Duke. And like I said that was only when he was off his face. The rest of us kept out of the way when that was going on. Like we knew Duke would act the next day as if nothing had happened. He'd even ask Raewyn, in our hearing, what she'd done to her face. But each time it happened I had this feeling, a sort of instinct, you know? That he could hurt her outside but he couldn't touch her on the inside. She was tough, see. She was made of something else besides flesh.

'Men,' she said to me one day, 'they're all the same. It's no different in the suburbs. I've lived there. I know. Sober, they're putty in your hands. But let them loose on the turps and they're wild bloody animals.'

'Not all of them,' I protested. 'Cutter just spews.'

'Cutter can turn evil just like the others,' Raewyn said. 'Ask Trudi.'

'So why do you live here then, if they're all such evil bastards?'

Raewyn gave me another of her looks. Then she said, 'How old are you kid?'

'Thirteen.' Actually I was still twelve at the time, but thirteen sounded better.

'You should be at school,' she said.

'Bugger school!' I said, grinning. 'School sucks!'

'Do you have any idea what you're getting into, Max?'

Well of course I told her to keep her shirt on, only I didn't use those words, you don't talk like that to Raewyn. But I made sure she got the message. I'd been in the gang six months. I knew what went on. And I knew about Trudi and Cutter too. How he'd brought these prospects home from the pool parlour one night, before I got here this was, and they'd put Trudi on the block. I didn't like to think about that, I mean Trudi had been good to me and I just didn't like to think . . . But I didn't want Raewyn seeing me as some half-arsed kid either.

That kinda brought things to a halt. In fact Raewyn didn't talk to me so much after that day. I was way past needing her help with the knitting and I was getting into stuff with the bros that kept me busy. But I did learn about Hine-nui-te-po. Only it wasn't Raewyn who enlightened me, it was Cutter, over a game of pool.

Pool was one of the other things I learned. Most nights the bros would go to this pool parlour in town. Sometimes there'd be a stoush if the local chapter of the White Knights, our main enemies, were out in force. But usually it was just us and a few of the local hoons.

I really liked pool. Got to be good at it too. I reckon if they had pool in this place no one would bother setting fire to his mattress.

'You heard of Maui?' Cutter asked me, during a lull in the game.

Well of course I'd heard of Maui. Wouldn't be standing here if it wasn't for Maui. He was the one fished Aotearoa out of the sea. But it wasn't that Maui Cutter wanted to talk to me about, but the one who met his match in Hine-nui-te-po, the goddess of death. 'Giver of life and taker of life, that's her,' Cutter told me. 'I tell ya Max, that's one lady ya wouldn't want to fuck with.'

Hine-nui-te-po lives in the underworld, which is where you go to join your ancestors when you die. That is if you're Maori. But if you're a Christian, which I am now, then you go to heaven. It's all a bit confusing, but I've worked it out. You go to Po, that's the underworld, for three days, like Jesus did when he descended into hell. Then you go to heaven, taking your ancestors with you. If I'm wrong I guess I'll find out. But I don't reckon I'm wrong.

One thing Duke wouldn't stand for and that was glue sniffing. He caught me at it one day and beat the living daylights out of me. I couldn't make it out. I mean he was always snorting things up his own nose. I couldn't see the difference between that and the glue. But he had this rule. No needles and no glue. If I didn't like it I could cut tracks.

117

I've sniffed glue in this place and reckon Duke was right. I mean it doesn't work the same as smoking. Don't get me wrong. Pare is hell. It makes other jails look like Disneyland. But if you can get your hands on a good porno mag and some grass you can make out like you're having the best of times. It don't take much to turn your home (that's what we call our cells) into a heaven. Only trouble is, it don't last.

The best thing I learned while I was in the gang, apart from how to look out for myself and the bros, was carving. It was Cutter taught me that too. He had this grouse set of tools and a heap of cow bone and paua shell to make things from. He carved in wood too but I wasn't into that so much. It was bone I liked working with, and shell. I made pendants and earrings and buckles for belts. I nicked this book about tribal motifs from the library and copied out the ones I liked. I learned a lot from that book, about what things meant and stuff. Carving's what I'm going to do when I get out of this place. Marama was always telling me I should flog my stuff to the tourist shops. But Marama's dead now. She died last Christmas. Cutter wrote me about it. Decent of him considering I'm a marked man these days. I've lost count of the number of beatings I've had since I decided to leave the Patus. I've even been beaten up by hoons from other gangs.

I haven't got my head round Marama's death yet. She was always pretty flakey but I never thought she'd do herself in. Not the way she did. Pills maybe, I could see that, but not cutting herself. Perhaps she was out of it on something and thought she was making a new tattoo. I've heard of that happening.

When I think of Marama now I see this stringy chick with plaits and gang tattoos on her cheeks. Two hearts pierced by the word Patu. They were always going septic those tats.

There was a lot of stuff went on. I'd be lying if I tried to say different. Most of our aggro came from the White Knights. They were a bikie gang, which we weren't. But that wasn't what made them our enemies. Tell you the truth I don't know what did, except that they were skinheads. They didn't call themselves that but that's what they were all right. They had Nazi insignia scrolled on their jackets and went round shouting Sieg Heil at everyone. If that doesn't make them skinheads then my name's not Maxwell Arapata Nene.

Come to think of it the White Knights were all Pakeha, which pretty much proves my point. Plenty of times they called us niggers. From a safe distance mind. But we had our answer ready when they did that. We'd turn our backs, drop our jeans, and give them the brown eye. After that fighting would come as a relief.

I guess the feeling was that everyone who wasn't on our side was an enemy, but with the White Knights it was war to the death.

At first I wasn't allowed anywhere near the scene of a fight. I mean with the White Knights we weren't talking fists, we were talking weapons. Knives and shotguns. We always knew when and where the stoush would take place. Like it was planned, the way it used to be when the English fought Napoleon. Mick ended up on a four year lag after one of these engagements. But that was no defeat. He'd put an end to the head honcho's career by blinding him. We counted that as a victory.

Like I said, I wasn't allowed to join in the fights, not till I was sixteen. All I was allowed to do for those first four years was deliver dope and make the odd raid on a shop. The first time the pigs caught me I was let off with a caution. I hadn't done much, maybe that was why, just hurled a rock through the window of this tourist outfit down by the lake. The pig who interviewed me talked a whole lot of bull about social responsibility and how he could see I was a bright lad, and did I really want to spend the rest of my life chucking rocks through windows? I thought for certain he'd rumble who I was, even with the false name Duke had dreamed up for me. But no. Reckon he was enjoying hearing himself talk too much to listen to anything I had to say. Not that I didn't have my story ready. Duke had me primed. I couldn't believe my luck! I mean, there I was, old enough to do time in borstal, if not some place worse, being let off with a sermon.

After that, Duke reckoned I was old enough to be part of the action. I knew what that meant. It meant I would have to prove myself, do something a bit more spectacular than robbing a kiosk or siphoning petrol.

My chance came one night after a drug run. Once a week or so I'd hike to this pad up in the hills to collect dope. At first I was allowed to take the dogs but that stopped once Shane took over. I complained to Duke, told him the dogs gave me protection, but he just laughed. 'Count yourself lucky those bloody flea carriers haven't got you busted yet,' he said. 'Talk about drawin' attention to yourself!'

It was after eight when I got back to the house. Winter so it was dark. I knew what was being planned. A rage to welcome some of the bros from the Morrinsville chapter. You could hear the music half a mile away.

I let myself in through the gate, talked to the dogs who still ran out to greet me despite Shane, and went into the kitchen. Raewyn, Marama, Trudi and a chick I didn't recognise were sitting round the table. You'd never have thought a party was going on from the looks on their faces. Raewyn, who had her head in her hands, looked up at me, blinked, and lowered her head again. I thought it must be the music that was getting to her — Sid Vicious and the Sex Pistols. I didn't go much on it either.

I made as if to move into the main room but Raewyn stopped me. 'You got the dope kid?' she asked.

'I'm not a kid.'

'Well pardon me! Give it here.'

It wasn't what was supposed to happen. I was supposed to hand it to Duke. But something in the way all four women were looking at me made me submit.

'Where's Shane?' I asked. Normally Shane would be the last person I'd ask for, but as he was the only other prospect living in the house at that time I reckoned I should be where he was. Something was going on and I didn't like the feel of it.

When no one answered me I went and got myself a beer. Returning to the table I saw that Trudi had made a space for me. I sat down, took a smoke off Marama, and before long I'd decided things were fine after all. The music was too loud and there was a sort of moaning sound like wind in a chimney which didn't seem to be part of the music but that was fine too. The kitchen began to take on an orangey glow. It made me think of Nan and her orange arms. I had another beer and then another and the joint was passed round and the room got warmer and I guess, in the end, I must have passed out.

I woke next morning to see Duke standing over me like the ghost of Hine-nui-te-po. I had no idea how I'd got to bed. The last thing I remembered was Nan's orange arms. 'You want to be patched up?' Duke asked me.

I nodded.

'Then I've got a job for you.'

I got up shakily and followed him downstairs. The kitchen was empty. I told him I needed to take a leak, but he ignored me and walked on into the main room. Shit! The place looked as if a bomb had been thrown into it. Two windows broken, the sofa practically ripped in two, blood and chuck on the carpet. I thought I was going to spew myself, with the smell and that, but I knew Duke was looking at me, testing me in some way, so I breathed as deep as I could through my mouth and looked back at him as if this was something I saw every day.

'OK, Max,' Duke said, 'this is how it goes. We had a rage here last night. One of the White Knights' chicks got caught up in the middle of it, if you get my meaning. We put her on the block which is where sluts like her deserve to be. But she got away. That motherfucker Rooster took his eye off the ball and she was gone. So there'll be some aggro. Bet your life on it. Meantime . . .' Duke bent down so that he could eyeball me. Then, lowering his voice, he said. 'In the old days the sheilas never narked. They knew the score. If they came to the pad they knew what would happen. But this bitch, this stupid cunt, she came here thinkin' she'd have a bitta fun. Off her face she was, away with the fuckin' fairies. But she sobered up soon enough when she saw what we had in mind for her. Are you with me so far?'

I nodded. My insides felt as if they'd had a bomb thrown at them. But I didn't look away. I was proud of myself for that.

'This is what I want you to do. You an' Shane. Stupid cunt'll scream and shout to the pigs, no question. She'll say there was a whole lot of us. But if you an' Shane . . .'

'Was he part of it?'

Duke grinned. 'Not that he remembers.'

'I was a prospect before him.'

'Exactly. That's why I'm talkin' to you like a bro.'

'Whadda you want me to do?'

'I want you to take the rap.'

I plunged my hand into my mouth but it was too late. Up came the chunder and spewed itself all over Duke's feet.

Duke stepped back, wiped his boots on the edge of the sofa, and repeated what he'd just said.

'Does it have to be with Shane?' I muttered, when I could trust myself to speak.

'Why?' Duke's smile was beginning to look menacing. 'Somethin' bad goin' on with you an' him?'

I shook my head. The taste in my mouth, and the stink in my nostrils, were so foul it was only a matter of time before I threw up again. 'No,' I whispered.

'That better be the truth,' Duke hissed.

I wrapped my hands around my chest. It was freezing that morning and all I had on were underpants and a T-shirt. Both of which smelt like shit.

'So here's what you do, Max,' Duke said, smiling normally again. 'When the pigs come round you tell them it was you, you an' Shane. You'll go down for it. I won't lie to you. But when you come out you'll be one of the brotherhood. You'll have the word Patu tattooed on your hands, you'll have the patches and you'll have the respect. Are you with me?'

'I'm with you,' I said.

And I was.

And Duke was right. I did two years that time. It wasn't good but it wasn't as bad as being in this place.

And when I came out I had the respect.

16

'Renate? It's Maggie. Have I woken you?'

'Actually I'm just on my way out.'

'You're an early bird.'

'I'm going to visit my mother.'

'Why I'm phoning . . . I wanted you to know . . .'

I wait. The silence is unnerving. 'Are you still there?' I ask.

'It's Greg. He's . . .'

So, I think, this is it. The call I've been expecting. Dreading. I wait for Maggie's voice, and that word, *dead*. Greg is dead.

Yesterday, re-reading Max's stories in the wake of my visit to Queenie's, hoping to find a clue as to what happened to him, something so obvious hit me I turned to his photo and shouted, 'Acting! You were acting. And I fell for it . . .'

It was his description of the morning after the rage that triggered it. He'd told me, on my first visit to Pare, that he couldn't remember what he'd done to land himself in prison. It was an impressive performance — the confused young criminal acknowledging a crime he couldn't remember committing. He wasn't inside for rape that time; he was inside for murder. But as I read his words, and thought about what they so vividly recalled, I knew this was a man who forgot nothing. And I understood something that had eluded me till then. Not being able to forget was part of Max's tragedy. Most of us are blessed with limited and highly selective memories. We forget the words we wish we hadn't spoken; the deeds we wish we hadn't committed. But Max, practised liar and consummate actor, forgot nothing.

'He's regained consciousness,' Maggie's voice says in my ear. 'He's going to be all right. He's going to live.'

'Oh dear God . . .'

'The doctors say . . .'

'I'm so glad,' I whisper, as her voice breaks again.

'Of course they can't be sure. But they think, well the prognosis is, no long-term damage . . .'

'That's wonderful. Absolutely wonderful. I told you, didn't I?'

'Tim's here. He flew up on Tuesday.'

'Give him my love.'

'And Alan's phoned every day from Sydney.'

'Good on him.'

'We've located Cressida too. I'm going to call her as soon as Greg's able . . .'

'Would you like me to come and see him?' I say to Greg's wife.

But I already know what her answer will be.

When the call is ended I sit very still, and stare at the phone. When Cecil died the phone never stopped ringing. I came to dread it: having to thank people for their sympathy; knowing they, like me, were angry he had died. Cecil never belonged to me. Perhaps that's why I didn't marry him. He belonged to the people who saw him as necessary to their survival. One of whom was ultimately responsible for his death.

But Greg is not going to die. Maggie, who needs him, can breathe again. And I, who needed him once, can get on with my life.

I walk out on to the balcony. Sunday morning. A lifeless grey day that does nothing to calm the erratic beating of my heart. Somewhere behind that immense shield of cloud the sun is shining. I imagine it struggling to break through, as Greg struggled to break out of his coma. But as always it's the casino tower that draws my eye. Standing like an exclamation mark above the monochrome city, it dwarfs even the stately Norfolk pines, whose crowns of frail crosses long ago caught the attention of missionaries.

In the distance, imagined not seen, lies the harbour. The day Greg and I were married the harbour was pure crystal. A perfect day in early summer. The ceremony took place in his house, on the front verandah overlooking the water, the glare so bright we had to wear dark glasses.

It was a small wedding; family and a few friends. Greg's mother and younger sister were there, as well as his three children. On my side there was my brother and his family and my mother. Out of deference to her we had a Presbyterian minister perform the ceremony. My mother would have preferred us to have had a service in an Anglican church, but that was too much for Greg to swallow.

Greg's son Tim was his witness. Mine was Tess, whose long red hair, garlanded with flowers, seemed to send out sparks in the afternoon sun. And that, with the addition of Tess' daughter, Caroline, and a couple of Greg's legal friends, was our entire guest list. It was what we'd both wanted, an intimate occasion, unobserved by strangers.

I look radiant in the photographs. Everyone says so. What I felt, as I said the words, as I made those amazing, defiant promises, was that I was saying them to Cecil too. I don't know whether, if Cecil and I had made those promises, they would have kept him alive, but I was determined not to take that risk with Greg. I never did tell Cecil he was necessary to my survival. Marrying Greg was my way of saying just that. Not that I wouldn't survive, physically, if he were to disappear or die, but the person I was in my marriage, *she* would not survive.

We went to Kawau Island for our honeymoon. In keeping with the radiant wedding photos, the honeymoon was idyllic. We ate oysters, drank champagne and made love as if we had only just discovered it and couldn't get enough of it. In between times we swam and read and planned a life that presented no obstacles to our continuing happiness.

'We'll have a crack at it as soon as we get back,' Greg promised, when, in the afterglow of a night's lovemaking, I felt confident enough to raise the subject of selling the house. 'You've got it looking shipshape now. And this is a good time to sell.'

But it didn't happen. There was a reason — there was always a reason — an important case; one of the kids coming to stay; a law conference to attend. After a while I stopped asking. I learned to live with the ghosts of past wives. I made my peace with the weeds and the work and the sense of isolation. But whenever I heard the word 'home' it wasn't Greg's house I saw, but a stone cottage on a Cornish cliff.

'It's not finished,' I hear Cecil say. 'And it won't be finished until . . .'

I spin round, but there's no one there. Just the curtains twitching in the breeze and the blurred outline of a room.

'Don't ever imagine Dad will do what *you* want,' Tim said to me, on one of his rare visits to the house. 'He may be a hotshot lawyer, but he's a total Neanderthal when it comes to human relationships.'

Tim is a lawyer himself. Following in his father's footsteps, as I was quick to point out that day. He even looks like his father, minus the eyes — Tim's are grey — and with the addition of a couple of inches.

'OK, so I'm trying to prove something,' Tim answered me, flashing his father's smile. 'But it's not what you think. I stopped trying to get my father's attention when I stopped wetting my bed. Why do you think Alan and I chose to stay with our mother? We could have lived with Dad once we were at secondary school. Not that he tried all that hard to persuade us. He was more concerned about scoring points over our mother. No, what *I* want to prove is entirely for my own benefit. And for my family's, if I ever have one. I want to prove you can be a hotshot lawyer *and* a decent human being.'

'That's not fair, Tim. Look at the work your father does. Look at the causes he supports.'

'Not talking about the public man,' Tim argued. 'Come on, Renate, you live with him. You know what I'm talking about.'

But I wasn't going to be drawn into that trap.

'What my father should have been is a monk,' Tim went on.

126

'With visiting rights to the local convent. The old boy needs women, but that doesn't mean he likes them. I'm afraid you're one in a long line, Renate.'

'The last in a long line,' I asserted firmly.

'Time will tell,' Tim said.

I shake my head in an effort to stop the flow of memories. Somewhere nearby a church bell rings, reminding me I should be on the road to Hamilton.

I move back inside, grab what I need, lock up the flat and head for the car. Two hours later I'm sitting in my mother's neat, clean, safe house. I've driven past the road I took the day before yesterday to visit Queenie. I've driven past the corner where Max was killed. If I also drove past the scene of Greg's accident, then I did so in ignorance.

The ghost who accompanied me on my journey was one I had tried earlier to banish. But this time his presence was curiously soothing. Greg in mellow mood could be an irresistible companion: discussing his latest case as we linger over a candle-lit dinner; stopping the car to show me a stand of kauri on one of our northern holidays, his voice humble as he contemplates nature's magnificence; peopling a hillside with tattooed warriors, directing my eye to the marks of warfare on an otherwise green and pleasant stretch of land; smiling at me across a room filled with our friends; asleep beside me, an arm cradling my breast, a leg holding me in the shape of our lovemaking. As I sit at my mother's table, eating macaroni cheese, I can feel his breath on my face. 'I adore you, Renate,' he whispers.

'Is it all right if I stay?' I ask my mother.

I don't need to hear her answer. It's as predictable as the seasons; as soothing as a scented bath. When I can no longer hold back my tears, my mother's arms are around me in a second, arresting my descent into the underworld, hauling me back on to the plain of her deep, unquestioning love.

'You're completely exhausted,' she tells me. 'And no wonder. That awful woman had no right to involve you like that. You've more than enough on your plate . . . That's it sweetheart, let it all out. You're safe here. You can rest as long as you want.'

When the fit has passed I let my mother lead me to my old bedroom, where I strip off my clothes and fall into a bed smelling of lavender. I don't remember anything after that. The sleep that comes to me is the sleep of an exhausted child.

When I wake Cecil is standing by the window, in the same nonchalant pose he adopted at the hospital. He smiles and holds up his left hand. Even though the room is in semi-darkness — my mother has drawn the curtains — I can see the gold ring on his third finger. Cecil, who never wore rings in life, seems to have acquired one in the afterlife.

I sit up, determined to question him, but get no further than the first syllable. 'Wh . . .'

Cecil lowers his hand, smiles at me again and disappears.

I fall back on the pillow. I realise from the light filtering patchily through my mother's curtains that it's still daytime. I swing my legs on to the floor, only to discover they no longer function. Could my mother have put something in my tea? The thought makes me laugh. A rogue thought from the pages of Max's life, not mine.

When the dizziness has passed I wrap myself in an eiderdown, move to the window and open the curtains. Sunlight streams into my mother's garden. Why have I never noticed its beauty before? After my father died all I wanted to do was escape this place. I hated Hamilton; hated the constant reminders that my father was gone. My mother kept the garden as his memorial. Was that why I was blind to it? Now I see in its stately trees, some of them still fiery with autumn leaves, and its borders bright with pansies and late roses, a sign of enlarging love, not continuing sorrow.

Out of sight, where the lawn falls away in a steep bank, is the Waikato River, once the boundary separating settler troops from their Maori foe. What would Max feel if he were standing here? Would he tell me? Or would he say what he thought I wanted to hear? That we understood each other; that we accepted our different pasts, known and unknown; that there existed between

128

us a miraculous communication, independent of the facts of history.

'But you never told me about Cecil,' I hear Max accuse. 'Or about your father.'

'I didn't realise I was supposed to,' I answer.

'Oh, I see, it was to be a one-way thing, was it? You were to find out about me, but I wasn't to know anything about you.'

'That's not true.'

'Isn't it?'

'You asked for my help, Max. That was how it all started.'

'And now you're asking for mine.'

I turn round eagerly, but the room is empty. 'Damn!' I say, out loud.

That night my mother and I sit by the fire and talk as we've never talked before. I'm not quite sure why this is. My mother knows almost nothing about Max. Or Greg for that matter. But what I come to see, as the clock ticks towards midnight, is that my mother has understood far more than I realised. She has always known, for instance, that I loved Cecil in the same way I loved my father. I never questioned or doubted the efficacy of that love. It existed like air or water, essentials to life.

'You never told me much about him,' my mother says. 'Your letters . . . well, it wasn't so much what you said as what you left out that made them interesting!' She laughs. 'But then, you see, I had your novels, and they told me so much more.'

'That's fiction, Mum. It's not the same as . . .'

'So who is Sebastian in *The Cornish View* if he's not Cecil?'

Now it's my turn to laugh. 'Mum, you're incorrigible,' I say.

We don't talk about Greg. I'm grateful. I want to go on feeling glad he's alive. I told my mother soon after I arrived that he'd regained consciousness and she hugged me wordlessly. I was grateful for that too.

Eventually I persuade her to say something about herself. It's not easy for her. She comes from a generation of women who regard self-examination as a close cousin to masturbation. But having drunk two glasses of wine, again at my persuasion, she begins to open up, with frequent pauses and far too many apologies.

I am amazed at what I hear. Her love for my father was passionate. When he died she nearly died herself, of anger and grief. But there was me and my brother Graham, the one so like her, the other so like the man she adored. 'You look even more like him now your hair has grey in it,' she tells me. 'How proud he would have been of you.'

'But he was an accountant,' I point out. Not that I want to argue with her portrait of me as my father's heir, but having fought all my life against sentimentality (something I succumb to all too easily) I can't let myself be comforted by an image of myself that would mean my father was still alive in me.

'You've studied history,' my mother answers. 'Your father grew up during the Depression. He watched his mother struggle to feed five children when there was no wage coming into the house. He could have been a writer, like you. It was nothing for him to read four books in a week. Ivy Compton-Burnett, Joseph Conrad, H.G. Wells, Rebecca West, Virginia Woolf, Thomas Hardy, the whole of Dickens — he devoured them all. I would say he needed literature as much as others need fresh air.'

'I remember him reading to us, I can still hear him describing Miss Haversham. And that moment when Pip first sees Magwitch in the graveyard . . .'

I stop, overcome by memories. I'm afraid that if I go on my father will materialize before me. What that would do to my mother I hardly dare imagine. The word *hallucination* is one she would consign firmly to a medical dictionary.

'I guess we'll never know whether he could have been a writer,' I say to her, 'but he could have been an actor, that's for sure.'

My mother smiles. 'And now there's you and your stories.'

'Do you know if he ever did write anything? Poetry, stuff like that. What about that desk of his, the one he kept locked? Did you find anything there?'

'Only documents,' my mother answers. 'His way of going

on loving us.' She smiles again. 'Everything was explained. In-vestments, insurance policies, details I might not have known about the house. A day doesn't go by when I'm not reminded how deeply, how thoroughly your father loved us. That's why I've never wanted to move.'

'So there was never any question . . . you were young when he died . . . You could have, you know . . . Dad wouldn't have minded.'

'No, but *I* would have.'

'That's sad.'

'I don't think so.'

'*I* married Greg.'

'Yes dear.'

'Are you telling me . . .'

My mother's eyes settle on mine. I'm not sure I like what I see reflected there. 'You are still writing, Renate?' she asks.

I take in a deep breath, sigh it out. Then I yawn. But it's no good. My mother's eyes continue to probe. 'I haven't for some time,' I admit. 'Not since . . .'

'Since your young friend died?'

'Before that.'

'Greg?'

I nod.

'That's over two years.'

I nod again.

'I don't think your father would like that,' she says quietly.

'Cut it out, Mum.'

She smiles. She used to call me a cheeky madam when I talked like that. Now, though I see the lines in her face and the white in her hair, we seem more like sisters than mother and daughter.

My mother's name is Amy. In the past, to annoy her, I'd some-times call her that. But it never got the reaction I wanted. My parents, Amy and George — between them they'd lived more than four decades before I came along. How arrogant of me to have imagined I knew them. But it seems love is not dependent on knowing. Is that what Max has been trying to tell me?

'I wonder if you know how important you are to me,' my mother says suddenly. 'No, that's not it. *Important* isn't the word. What I'm trying to say is, I wonder if you and your brother know how much I love you? I know you don't tell me half of what's going on in your lives, but that doesn't mean I'm not involved. There's not an hour goes by when I don't think of you both, you writing at your desk; Graham, with his tools and plans. I know you have to do other things to earn your living now, I know your early novels are out of print. But if you don't write, Renate, if you give it up altogether, you'll never find what you're looking for.'

'Who says I'm looking for anything?' I don't mean to sound petulant. I'm just not in the mood for interrogation.

My mother leans out of her chair to stoke the fire. I watch her irritably. *I* should have done that. 'I can be busy about many things, my dear,' she answers me. 'Not just charity work.'

'Mum . . .'

'The Busy Widow. Isn't that what you and Graham call me?'

I pick up a cushion and cover my face. It's what I used to do as a child when caught out in a lie. My mother laughs and I let the cushion fall. My mother's face is pink from the fire. I see her as a young woman suddenly, surprised by passion. I want to tell her I love her, but already she is talking again, deflecting attention away from herself.

'Your young friend,' she says. 'The one who died. You're grieving for him, aren't you?'

I nod. I don't trust myself to speak.

'Tell me about him.'

'He was very good at knitting,' I mutter.

'Knitting?'

'Yes.'

We look at each other solemnly. Then, as if someone has flicked a switch, we start to laugh. We laugh noisily, messily, blowing our noses and sniffing loudly. When it's finished, we sit back in our respective chairs and savour our mutual exhaustion.

'We should go to bed,' I say.

'When you've told me about Max,' my mother answers.

'It's late.'

'And I know you. You'll clam up again tomorrow, in the cold light of day.'

'Is that how you see me? I'm a writer, Mum. I can't afford to be emotionally repressed.'

'Exactly,' my mother says.

'Repression is *your* thing. Your generation, not mine. My contemporaries . . .'

'Max,' my mother insists.

'I don't know where to start,' I protest.

But it turns out I do. The words come tumbling out of me, in no particular sequence, words of frustration and fascination; of disappointment and pride; of love and anger and incomprehension. Greg gets mixed up in it, but I don't attempt to explain. By the time I've finished the wood has run out and the fire is no more than a faint glow.

My mother doesn't speak for a while. I take a peek at her to check she hasn't fallen asleep. She sees what I'm doing and smiles. 'These stories of Max's,' she says, 'the ones he wrote for you. Do you think they're true?'

'Absolutely,' I answer. 'That was the thing about him, what marked him out as a writer. He could *speak* lies, but he couldn't write them. Writing is about truth.'

'So the answers to your questions, the ones you tell me you're asking about him, will be in his stories.'

I look at my mother with what can only be described as astonishment. How does she know these things? I've said nothing about my recent revelation: that Max lied to me that first morning in Pare; that the truth could only be found in his stories. 'Yes,' I acknowledge. 'Some of it anyway.'

'Not out there with his family or the gang or — what was that man's name? The driver of the car?'

'Roy Harawira.'

'Him.'

133

'But . . .'

'If you weren't chasing after the facts of Max's life and death you'd be writing, wouldn't you?'

'Maybe.'

My mother leans across to touch my arm. I notice the brown spots on the back of her hands. They remind me of Cecil's freckles. 'Can I give you some advice?' she says.

'Of course.'

'Start writing again. Keep up the search if you must, but write about what's happening to you. Now. Each day. Write out of your vulnerability, Renate. Don't disguise it, like Max tried to.'

'You think that's what he was doing?'

'Why else would he have gone back to his old life?'

'We don't know he did that. There could be a perfectly innocent explanation.'

My mother's raised eyebrows irritate me. You don't know everything, I want to say to her. You never even met Max.

'That word *shame*,' she says. 'You said he used it a lot. You felt it meant something different to him, something darker. But if that was the case, wouldn't he have tried to re-invent himself in his writing? To mask that shame.'

'How do I know he didn't?'

'Re-inventing isn't the same as telling the truth, Renate.'

'Now you're contradicting yourself.'

My mother shakes her head. 'All I'm trying to say,' she insists, 'is that it's *your* truth you should be looking for, not Max's. Isn't that why you've come to see me?'

Again I look at her in astonishment. Has living on her own made her psychic? Or is it mother-love that gives her these powers? 'Since when has a daughter needed a reason to visit her mother?' I mutter.

She grins at me. As a child I used to think she was a witch, cursed (as far as I was concerned) with the power of x-ray vision. She could literally see what I was thinking. But she doesn't look like a witch now. With her hair, usually so neat, falling about her face, she looks like a softer, sweeter Germaine Greer. She's always done her hair the same way: waved softly at the front to cover her ears; caught up in a whorl at the back. It's always been long, always been thick, unlike mine, which is fine and flyaway. 'Getting back to Max,' she says, her tone reassuringly matter-of-fact. 'To his sense of shame. Isn't that just another way of saying *original sin*?'

'You don't believe in that, do you? I know you're a good Anglican, but . . .'

'You think we're born good, do you? That we only become bad because of society?'

'Well no . . .'

'Human beings aren't good, Renate. In fact I'd say there's more evil in the world than there is goodness.'

'Mum!' I protest, laughing. 'I had no idea you were such a cynic.'

'Oh, I'm not a cynic,' she assures me.

'You sound like one.'

'No more than your Max.'

I laugh again. 'I don't think you and Max . . .'

'But that's where you're wrong,' she interrupts. 'Max would know precisely what I was talking about. His shame, my original sin, they're the same thing. He may have seen further into the darkness than I have, but he won't stay there. No one does. That's why you keep imagining you see him. He wants to set you free so he can get on with his journey. And you' — she smiles at me — 'can get on with yours.'

I close my eyes. I feel if I look at my mother any longer her smile will burn me up. 'How do you know all this?' I ask, opening my eyes again.

Her smile widens. 'Because you've just told me,' she answers. 'You and Max.'

17

Cecil died on 3 April 1985. April is the cruellest month . . .

The day of his death we'd planned a walk in Kensington Gardens. A sudden warm spell had brought the daffodils out, eclipsing the snowdrops and crocuses which had cheered our city life till then. Cecil had the day off. I had a deadline to meet and needed to work through till lunchtime. The arrangement was that he would come to my place, have a bite to eat, then we'd take the bus to Kensington. But by lunchtime Cecil was dead.

If I'd given up my morning's work, if I'd done what my heart and my hormones wanted and spent the whole day with him, he would still be alive. Back in 1985 a day off meant just that. Away from his flat, Cecil would have been uncontactable. But Cecil was at home that morning. Reading the first draft of my new novel, as it happened. Planning, no doubt, what he would say to me about it as we walked amongst the daffodils.

At first, when the call came, I couldn't understand what was being said. I thought Robert, Cecil's partner, was trying to tell me Cecil had been called to the scene of an accident. That sort of thing was always happening. Patients, even other doctors, would ask for Cecil first, knowing he would come if he possibly could, he was that kind of man.

Then Robert started babbling about his wife, Daphne. She was on her way round, he said. I wasn't to do anything till she arrived. 'But I won't be here,' I said. 'Cecil and I . . .'

That's when I heard that word again. *Accident*. 'There's been an accident,' Robert interrupted me. 'Please, Renate. Try and stay calm.'

'What are you talking about? Who . . .'

'Daphne will . . .'

'Has something happened to Cecil?'

'I'm afraid so, yes.'

'But he's at home. We're meeting in an hour. He's at home.'

'He was called out . . . Or rather, he had a visitor.'

I remember the stab of anger I felt then. I'd lost count of the number of arrangements Cecil and I had made, only to have our plans scuppered by a phone call. The phone was one of the reasons we never lived together. At Cecil's place it never stopped ringing.

'Did Cecil ever talk to you about Arthur Woodham?' Robert asked.

Another stab, this time of panic. I felt as if I was watching a movie that had been speeded up. Try as I might I could not follow the plot.

Of course I remembered Arthur Woodham. One of Cecil's failures.

'The schizophrenic?' I said.

'Yes.'

'I thought he was in hospital.'

'He was. He got out. That is, he was discharged. Into the community. It's happening all the time now.'

'Cecil liked Arthur.'

'Cecil likes most people.'

'He's all right, isn't he? Robert? You're not phoning to tell me . . .'

'Arthur came round to Cecil's flat. It seems he'd convinced himself Cecil was his brother. He, well if you know the story you'll know he tried to kill his brother once . . .'

'The doorbell's ringing.'

'That'll be Daphne.'

'You're telling me Cecil's dead, aren't you, Robert? You're telling me Arthur Woodham killed him.'

137

There should have been an explosion at that point. The heavens should have opened, or the roof fallen in on my head. But there was just the doorbell, persistent as toothache, and Daphne, her face blurred with anxiety, her arms flailing as she reached out to me.

Yes, Arthur Woodham killed my love, but he is not the only one to stand accused. Cecil wanted us to live together. He never stopped wanting it. I was the one who objected. My work, the phone, his work. Whereas the truth was, while he accepted and even embraced the often self-inflicted demands of my working life, I never did the same for him. If we'd been together Arthur would either have failed in his purpose, or killed us both.

I didn't attend Arthur's trial. A verdict of insanity returned him to the institution that had ejected him only months before. So there are three guilty parties here: Arthur himself; the Government, whose policies were responsible for Arthur's release; and me.

The Christmas before Cecil's death he gave me a ring. It had belonged to his grandmother. A thin gold band encrusted with seed pearls. I thought it the loveliest thing I'd ever seen; far too lovely to wear. After Cecil died I went to look for the ring in my jewellery box. It had vanished. I turned my flat upside down, but I never found it. I shed more tears for that ring than I did for Cecil himself. I needed to have something of his, something tangible I could keep with me. I kept telling myself to choose his glasses, or his favourite coffee mug, or his old university scarf, which still carried his smell, but only that ring would do.

Cecil's funeral was, as everyone kept telling me, an uplifting affair. He wasn't a Christian but somehow, when it came to it, we gave him a Christian burial. His mother wanted it. That was part of it. And in the end there didn't seem to be any other way of doing it.

Cecil's ashes were scattered from the headland in Cornwall on which our cottage stood. I hadn't expected his mother to agree, but not only did she give her consent, she came with me.

It was more than I could bear to stay in the cottage, so we put up in a hotel in Looe.

I didn't know Cecil's mother very well then, but any fear I may have had that we would be awkward with one another was banished within an hour of leaving London. Like my own mother, Beth was a widow — a factor, I'd always assumed, in her depression. But at the end of those three days I understood what Cecil had so often been at pains to explain to me, that his mother's depression was chiefly due to her overly sensitive nature. So many things distressed her: the spread of Aids; child labour in the Third World; the plundering of the English countryside. Which made her strength during that time all the more remarkable. I was the one who broke down and wept when it came to the moment of farewell. I was the one who had to be helped back to the car. Beth, who had lost her only son, stood on that cliff like a warrior queen; noble, proud and courageous.

We scattered the ashes at night. Though it wasn't the holiday season there were enough people about to deter us from conducting the ritual during the day. I'd already shown Beth the cottage. She'd stood with her arm about me, silent in her sympathy, while the gulls wheeled above our heads and the wind tugged at our hair. When we came back, after the sun had gone down, the cottage was shrouded in darkness. I was glad it was uninhabited. I wanted it to belong to Cecil and me; to the ghosts of our past.

The ashes were in a copper urn, no bigger than a coffee mug. Beth had been holding it in the car, but as we walked across the springy turf to the cliff edge, she handed it to me. I looked up at the sky, wishing for stars, but there were only scattered pinpricks of light, emerging from behind the chasing clouds. Below me, concealed by the contour of the land, was the lighthouse. Its beams sliced the sea, revealing, for a brief moment, white-tipped waves and the tangle of rocks at our feet.

I don't know how long I stood, feverishly clutching the urn, like a child refusing to release a cherished toy. It may only have been a few seconds, but it felt much longer. I remember a feeling of calm descending on me, and with it the conviction that every-thing was going to be all right: everything *was* all right. But when Beth touched my arm and I lifted the urn high above my head, my conviction failed and I was gripped by a sense of loss so devastating I fell to my knees. It was left to Beth to finish what I had failed to do. 'God bless you,' I heard her say, as all that was left of my love was carried away on the wind. 'God keep you safe.'

I have a folder — it's lying on the desk in front of me now — which contains the letters Beth has written to me over the years; the newspaper reports of Cecil's death; and the letters of con-dolence, hundreds of them, which I received in the weeks after Cecil died. It seems he significantly affected almost everyone he met, for the better. He didn't just heal, one correspondent wrote, he *transformed*.

I had difficulty with all that praise. I wanted to remember Cecil as he really was: a nicotine-addict who wore odd socks; a short-sighted, long-haired, pointillist painting on two legs; a good man, a truly good man, but one who could be both absent-minded and stubborn.

I should have shown the folder to Greg. I see that now. I did try once, but his lack of interest so distressed me I never raised the subject again. Nor did I ever talk to him about Beth. She's dead now and Greg is out of my life. But I should at least have tried. My mother was right to worry about my clamming up. It's what I do when I fear rejection. 'Write out of your vulner-ability,' she instructed. The way she spoke, she made it sound easy. 'But you don't know what you're asking,' I answer her now, thinking of that bleak cliff, and Beth's words carried away on the wind.

I stare at the folder, with its cargo of memories, and try to remember exactly what I did promise my mother. I didn't say I *would* start writing again. Just that I'd try. But how am I to do that when I barely earn enough as it is? OK, so I've not been at my desk all that much lately. I've been chasing Max's story when I should have been chasing editing jobs. But if Mum's right, and the story I have to write is the one with me in it, then I haven't been wasting my time. Because I do need to understand what's been going on for me these last few years. Not just with Max. With Greg. With Cecil. With myself.

I get up from the desk and wander over to the bookcase. I'm not aware of any particular motivation, but when I get there I pull out a copy of *The Cornish View*. The mere sight of its cover, with its stylised depiction of the house that stands at the centre of the story, is enough to plunge me back into melancholy. What was I thinking when I wrote it? I know what I was thinking when I started, that I wanted to celebrate what I believed was a unique relationship. Despite keeping to many of the facts of my life with Cecil — our professions, for example — I believed I had created two *fictional* characters. That Sebastian, while resembling Cecil, had an independent life of his own. Likewise Donna. The trouble is, I'm not sure, in retrospect, that I like Donna very much; and I find Sebastian ever so slightly priggish.

So where does this leave my conviction that writing is about truth? A revised version of the novel was re-published two years after Cecil died. That this edition, far more closely autobiographical than its predecessor, was singled out for praise, is one of the reasons it took me so long to return to fiction. The boundaries had become too blurred. I no longer knew what kind of writer I was.

I slide my fingers lovingly over the jacket. 'Home,' I whisper. But I don't open the book. One day perhaps, if — when — I write the novel my mother wants, I'll risk re-reading it. In the meantime it will stand alongside my other mostly out-of-print novels, all of them autobiographical, according to one critical theory, but none of them remotely resembling *The Cornish View*.

The windows of my flat are closed, but the persistent sounds of the city still manage to creep into my consciousness. If I listen carefully I can separate out the steady swoosh of passing cars; the rise and fall of voices; a bell warning of the approach of a suburban train; and a throbbing noise I can't identify, but imagine to be some kind of pump. Then I hear a sound that doesn't belong in that discordant city symphony — the confident croak of a tui, announcing prematurely (the day is warm, like that day in April) the arrival of spring. As I listen to the tui's exuberant predictions, I feel a surge of something I have to call — no other word will do — joy.

I open the balcony doors, breathe in the jasmined air, and start to dance, self-consciously at first, but then more recklessly. The music in my head is Beethoven's 'Ode to Joy'. I make no attempt to hum it. The melody has been part of me for as long as I can remember. Max loved Beethoven; though when he first heard Mahler he said *he* was the greater composer. Max loved rap too, and the blues, though he never had much time for rock. Mozart he couldn't get along with at all. 'What that dude needed was to get high,' he said to me once. 'He's too bloody polite.'

Is Max in the room with me now? Is Cecil? Cecil was an enthusiastic dancer. He wasn't very good, but that never stopped him. The only thing he didn't like was dancing on his own. 'Crazy,' he'd say to me. 'Dancing is about contact. What's the point of being with you if I can't touch you?'

When the music in my head has ended, I collapse on the sofa and wait for the city noises to re-establish themselves. The train has gone and the tui is silent, but everything else is as before. I think of Beethoven, sitting down after years of deafness to compose his Ninth Symphony. The finale — the unsurpassable 'Ode to Joy' — was inspired by Schiller's poem of the same name. But words alone cannot account for that gloriously defiant celebration of life. Beethoven never saw a stand of kauri. He never even saw the sea. But everything in Nature existed in his imagination. Is Nature then the place to look for joy? Is that what Greg was trying to tell me when he led me into the heart of the kauri forest?

'Evil,' I read years ago, researching for a play I'd been commissioned to write, 'is the attempt to transform the terrible passivity of suffering into violent activity. It stems from the feeling of dread, from the fear of nothingness. In inflicting pain on others the sufferer, invariably a person adrift in the world with no place to call his own, is temporarily freed from that crippling feeling of dread.'

The words impressed me so much I committed them to memory. At the time I thought it an apt description of the fascist personality, exactly what I needed for my play. It made sense to me to see evil as stemming from a vacuum, not, as some theologians would still have us believe, originating in the mind of that variously named creature, Satan.

But that was before I knew Max.

Why am I thinking of this now? Is it because of the joy? The dance? Or is it because I need to test the theory against the continuing reality of Maxwell Arapata Nene? An outcast from the day he was born, a man tormented by dread, there's no doubt Max did evil things. He admits as much in his writing. What those crimes were is not the point. He did what he did to conquer the dread. In the part of him that was not contaminated he knew his actions were wrong, bad, evil. But — and this is what I didn't, couldn't, know when I wrote my play — he almost certainly had no choice. Choice is an attribute of *my* world, the world of belonging. In the universe inhabited by Max and his kind, the word is meaningless.

You don't want to believe everything you hear about gangs, Renate. A lot of the time, most of the time, we're just getting on with our lives, like other people. Once I was patched up I could do pretty much what I liked: play pool; watch footie; visit mates; make out with any chick I fancied. I even got a job for a while, working with Hemi on a building site.

But in 1984, after a bail-up that went wrong, I landed back inside. I wasn't taking the rap. This one was for real. The shotgun I pointed at Rama Patel was loaded. I'd have used it too, if I'd had to. Which was what I told Duke when he paid me a visit in gaol. 'Pity you didn't use it on the pig that busted you,' he commented. 'Killing pigs is the highest order of achievement, Max. Brings you a lotta grief, but when you see how the bros respect you, well, it compensates. Believe me, it compensates.'

'Have you ever killed a pig?' I asked. I knew he had. It was how he got his mana. But I wanted to hear him say it.

'I was lucky,' Duke answered. 'I never got done for it.'

I knew then what I was going to do. Sooner or later I would kill a pig. I was ambitious, see. I didn't want to be just another patched member. I wanted to be Duke's son and heir.

And you know something? Every time I thought of it I knew how easy it was going to be. I had a dozen personal reasons to hate pigs. Times when I'd been stopped in the street for no reason at all, then pushed up against a wall and searched. Times when I'd been dragged from my car and beaten up. Times when I'd been hit during questioning so as not to leave a bruise. More times than I can count when I'd been called names like nigger and wog and kumera cruncher. One sweaty young pig, trying to outdo his mates, called me a curry-muncher, which is a bit of a laugh considering I hate Asians.

It would be just like in the war. That's what I told myself. Soldiers were trained to go into a bayonet charge thinking of someone they hated. No one objected when they killed Germans. Some of them even got medals.

'The answers to your questions,' my mother said, 'will be in Max's stories.'

Is that why I'm reading them again now? Is it possible to see the dark and the light as one? To understand the mystery in a single, comprehending flash? Is that why I'm still gripped by joy?

Them and us. How many times have I heard that phrase? *I* belong to the decent, law-abiding world; Max was one of *them* — the criminal underclass. Yet in my world I am a daily witness to legally sanctioned acts of greed and selfishness, some of which I would describe as evil; while in Max's world I have seen with my own eyes deeds of kindness, love and generosity. If Max was sitting by me he'd tell me the two worlds were one; his just the mirror image or shadow of mine. But Max isn't sitting by me. I have to do this part of the journey on my own.

Perhaps, I think, as I run my hands over the cover of his

exercise book, I should let my mother read these stories. She is a Christian, like Max. She may be able to explain why I cannot condemn him. Why, even now, struggling to piece together the jigsaw of his life, it's not his crimes I'm interested in, but *him*.

Had the dread got hold of him again when he got into that stolen car? Is that why he died? Or was he just bored? Max had a low boredom threshold. Mainly, I believe, because he was so intelligent, and so woefully under-educated. Being locked up with nothing but his own thoughts to distract him must have been a torment.

When he was released he had so many plans. He was going to study, with a view to going to university. He was going to improve his Maoritanga. He was going to help young people; warn them off drugs and alcohol and gang life. He was going to develop his carving; turn it into a business. But he did none of these things. Income Support wouldn't fund his study. I went with him to argue his case but it was hopeless. 'Encourage him to study part time,' I was advised. 'Plenty of people do it while holding down a job.'

I pointed out that getting a job wasn't going to be easy for Max. How many employers would take on a tattooed ex-crim with known gang connections? Max, listening to my indignant protests, touched my arm and smiled.

That was the beginning of a time, lasting right up to his death, in which, either separately or together, we scoured the employment columns of newspapers and notice boards. First came the gardening job; followed, when that failed, by a series of dead-end positions, most of which *I* drew Max's attention to. At different times he was a road sweeper, a telephone salesman, a fish-and-chip-shop worker, a petrol pump attendant. I tried not to let him see how profoundly discouraged I was by all this. He was discouraged enough himself. 'Once you've shown you can hold down a job, Income Support will change their mind about your education, you'll see,' I kept telling him.

But of course Max couldn't hold down a job. He didn't want to. Didn't see the point. He knew it was hopeless. In the largely

Pakeha world of work and learning he would always be one of *them*.

So, inevitably, the dread returned. Gradually, I imagine, not all at once. When Max asked to borrow my car he would have been feeling nothing for me. That was why, when I refused, he stayed silent. It wasn't makutu. His silence wasn't directed at me. It was directed at the monster inside him.

18

The day I suggested to Max that he might like to accompany me to a Beethoven piano recital, I expected him to react enthusiastically. What I didn't expect was to be lifted off my feet and clasped in a bear hug. 'Would I, hell!' he shouted. 'Renate, you're the greatest.'

Max's love of classical music began during his last lag in Pare. Apart from the times when he was in solitary, he was allowed a radio in his cell. Listening to the concert programme was something that started accidentally. Flicking through the stations, searching for the sports channel, he happened to hear the beginning of Beethoven's 'Violin Concerto'. By the time it ended he was well on the way to becoming a fan. As he would be, subsequently, on hearing Mahler. Others who made it into his personal Top Ten were Brahms, Shostakovitch and Bruckner. Opera he couldn't listen to. It made him giggle. And Schubert, my own personal favourite, he pronounced — to my intense annoyance — 'weedy'!

I didn't discover this passion till towards the end of his time in prison. I was there to teach him about writing, not music. But when I let slip that I once had teenage dreams of a musical career, there was no stopping him. I was quizzed about every new piece of music he heard. Nothing escaped his attention. If he heard a symphony by Philip Glass, or Michael Tippett, or our own Gareth Farr, he wanted to know where those particular sounds came from, and how they connected back to Beethoven. 'You must follow up on this when you get out,' I told him. 'Take lessons. Who knows? You might even be the next Michael Houston . . .'

Inevitably, like all my other dreams for Max, this one came to nothing. How could it? As he once bitterly pointed out, he barely had enough money to live on. Where would he get the cash to buy a piano? How the hell would he pay for lessons?

But at the time of my invitation, Max's life was going well. He was living with Pete. He had a job in a New Lynn garage. He even had a car, lent to him by his boss — a monstrous great silver thing, with flashy tyres and a broken silencer. His offer to come and pick me up was accompanied by his trademark grin. He knew how much I hated drawing attention to myself. Nevertheless I accepted gratefully. I'd not long since moved into my flat and was still feeling bruised and battered by the speed of my exit from Greg's life. To think I'd hoped the two men might be friends — that only a few months earlier I'd tried to persuade Greg to accompany me to see Max's kapahaka group. What the people from my former world, some of whom were bound to be at the concert, would make of my turning up at the Maidment Theatre with a tattooed Maori young enough (if I'd started early, like Queenie) to be my son, didn't really concern me. I'd learned to keep my relationship with Max separate from my workaday world. The only person I ever talked to about Max was Tess.

Max arrived early. He was wearing khaki trousers with pockets plastered all over them like letter boxes. His jacket was the one I'd bought for him on his release — green denim with silver studs. I suspected his black boots, laced halfway up his lower leg, were stolen goods. It happened all the time in Pare. Someone would steal an inmate's Reeboks. That inmate would in turn steal his neighbour's boots. When I asked Max why these thefts weren't reported, he just laughed.

'No complaints about my hair then?' he challenged, when I complimented him on his appearance.

'Always room for improvement,' I shot back at him.

We drove noisily into town, parked as near as we could to the university and walked along the leafy, brightly lit street to the theatre. Max, who always had some adventure to recount, told me about his latest drama. Driving home from work the previous night he was stopped by the cops, ordered out of his car and forced to lean over the roof while they searched him.

'What were you doing?' I asked, interrupting his indignant narrative.

'Nothing,' he answered.

'You must have been doing something. Was it the broken silencer?'

Max gave me a pitying look. 'You don't get it, do you, Renate? It's nothing to do with broken silencers. It's never about stuff like that.'

I decided not to pursue the subject. I didn't want Max walking into the theatre looking as if he was about to start the revolution. So I took his arm and launched into a tale of my own, one I knew would interest him because it involved the sonatas we'd come to hear. Only later did it occur to me I'd let an opportunity pass. At the very least I should have let him know I understood what he was saying, and felt as indignant about it as he did.

As we approached the door a familiar nervousness gripped me. Since the dramatic end of my marriage I'd been finding it increasingly difficult to go out into the world. The fear of encountering Greg and Maggie, arms locked around each other, infected me with a kind of paralysis. So far it had happened only once, outside the Public Library. Maggie had stared at me a moment, then burst out laughing. Greg had looked embarrassed. But they won't be here tonight, I consoled myself. Greg's taste in classical music began and ended with 'Eine Kleine Nachtmusik'.

Once we'd taken our seats, Max fell silent. I glanced at him from time to time, but felt shy of intruding on whatever it was he was thinking. This was his first classical concert. For all I know he'd never even seen a grand piano before. I don't think it was the audience that was affecting him. Strangers never bothered Max. Nor did crowds. If anything I was the one who was uneasy. I'd recognised a few faces when we arrived, but made no attempt to approach anyone. I wasn't ashamed to be seen with Max. I'd hardly have taken his arm if that had been true. But I wanted to keep this evening about music: not about the police stopping cars; or my middle-class acquaintances seeing me on Max's arm and stopping in their tracks.

The concert lived up to both our expectations. There were two pianists, both final year students at the School of Music. The first half was taken up with 'The Hunt', not one of my favourite sonatas, but vigorously played, with only a few rough patches. The ever-popular 'Moonlight Sonata' occupied the second half. Max, who'd never heard it before, didn't want to talk when it was over. Perhaps, like me, he hoped its haunting melodies would linger in his mind. But I suspect it was more to do with the sense of longing that particular piece of music invariably awakens.

What were you longing for that night, Max? I wonder now. And what did you mean when you told me, on the way home in your noisy silver car, that you loved me? And why — why, why, why — was there never another occasion like that? You never came to any more concerts with me. No matter how hard I tried to persuade you. And you never used that word 'love' again.

Why?

19

Six weeks pass. I work diligently at my editing, confident I am, at least in part, keeping my promise to my mother. The extraordinary rush of joy I felt after my visit to Hamilton has not returned, but the memory of it continues to buoy me. I'll be rewriting a sentence, agonising over where to put a comma, when suddenly my concentration goes and I find myself smiling into the empty room. I'm not consciously looking for Cecil, or Max, but I'm certain they're both there. In more fanciful moments I imagine them watching me, winking at one another when I do something predictable.

The unanswered questions about Max continue to trouble me, but I seem to have managed to distance myself from them. I tell myself I'm waiting, like Max's family, for the coroner's report. But it's more than that. Reluctant though I am to admit it, I've begun to accept I may never find the answers.

I think what I'm experiencing is a period of incubation. It's the time that comes before the writing starts; a brooding time when all doors are open and anything is possible. Some writers describe it as a *cerebral pregnancy*, but I prefer to think of it as a time of waiting and listening. It's the best part of the writing process. That's what I used to tell my students when poverty forced me to take up teaching after Cecil's death. When I found I could no longer write.

I told my mother about what seems to be going on for me, and her relief that I was at last beginning to see myself as a writer again made me feel ashamed of all the years I've spent not confiding in her. Each time I come off the phone to her I realise I no longer feel as lonely. Whether this is because of our growing intimacy, or because I continue to feel the nearness of Max and Cecil, I'm not sure. Both probably. And at least, in sceptical moments, I can reassure myself that even if Max and Cecil are illusions, my mother is not.

I've also talked to Maggie. Ever since the day she called to tell me Greg had regained consciousness, I've felt inhibited about phoning. My suggestion, at the end of that call, that I might visit again, was received coolly. I realised Maggie needed to distance me from Greg. Nevertheless I felt I had a right to know if the prediction of no long-term damage had been correct. 'It's too soon to know for sure,' Maggie informed me, 'but the omens are good.'

I felt sad as I said goodbye, but not bitter. 'It *is* finished,' I said, confident Cecil could hear me. 'I know that now.'

By the end of the six weeks I've caught up on my work and paid the most pressing of my bills. Now is the moment when I should open a new file on my computer, label it 'Novel: Working Title: *Loving Max*' and see what has been hatched in the incubation period. But that isn't what I do. What I do is ring Pete, something I've been putting off ever since my visit to Queenie's. I can't explain why I've procrastinated. There was a time when I thought Pete and I were united in wanting to find answers.

'Been wondering what you've been up to,' Pete says.

'Work mainly,' I explain. 'And thinking about Max. About those answers we were going to try and find.'

'Any luck your end?'

'Nothing tangible, I'm afraid.'

'Reckon I might have somethin',' Pete says.

My throat contracts painfully. 'Vincent told me about the Filofax,' I confess. 'I should have phoned sooner, but . . .'

'Filofax is only part of it,' Pete interjects.

I cover my mouth with my hand. How could I have left it so long? How could I have imagined I could write anything with so many unanswered questions hanging over me? My mother was wrong. Understanding Max is more important than understanding myself.

'Whadda you doin' tonight?' Pete asks suddenly. 'Can you come over?'

Which is how, two hours later, I get to be crawling through commuter traffic, en route to Pete's house in New Lynn.

Pete lives in the same sort of ramshackle dwelling as Queenie: a former State house, now controlled by a corporation. Pete is a sickness beneficiary; his asthma makes it impossible for him to work.

Also living there is Alan, a recovering alcoholic, an old man named Sean, who appears to be suffering from dementia and Tipper, an ex-inmate.

I've anticipated Pete and I might not have the living room to ourselves, but we do. Alan is out at an A.A. meeting, Sean is asleep and Tipper, Pete tells me, hasn't been seen for days. 'Between you, me an' the gatepost,' he confides, 'I reckon he's on the run.'

The last time I came to this house Max was still alive. Tipper has his room now. I glance down the passage and see the door is closed. Trying not to imagine that room, with its cargo of books and clothes and Pacific Art posters, only makes it more vivid. As if they were spread out in front of me, I see the saucers Max used as ashtrays; the plastic holdall he converted to a knitting bag; the carving tools I gave him last Christmas, still in their packaging; the headphones next to his bed; the exercise books in which he scribbled his increasingly private thoughts.

I imagine the police removed those exercise books when they searched the place after Max's death. The fact that I don't know what he'd written in them is a cruel reminder of how far apart we'd grown. Once I would have been invited to read everything he wrote.

'You wanted to see Max's Filofax,' Pete says.

'What was he up to, Pete? Lily seemed to think he was setting up a business of some kind. Did you know about that?'

Pete gets up from his chair. His breathing isn't good tonight.

I used to tell Max he shouldn't smoke in Pete's house, but Pete swore smoking had nothing to do with his asthma. 'Doctor reckons it's household dust,' he insisted. 'I'm fine outside.'

'There's something you should see,' he says now, nodding towards the kitchen. I pick up the bags of food and beer I brought with me and follow him out of the living room.

As we step onto the ragged linoleum my face contracts in an involuntary grimace. A horrible smell is emanating from the overflowing rubbish bin in the corner. And that's not all. Unwashed dishes cover the bench. Fly spots decorate the walls and the green plastic light shade, giving them the appearance of diseased flesh. As for the stove, it seems to be covered in orange blisters. When Max lived here the kitchen was kept clean.

Pete opens a cupboard and takes out an object that looks like a Bunsen burner. 'I managed to hide this from the cops,' he announces proudly.

'What is it?'

'It's what Max was using to cook up.'

I shake my head. It's not that I don't know what 'cooking up' means. I knew people in London who were into this sort of thing. But why this elaborate contraption? Couldn't Max have made do with a candle?

'That was the business Max was getting into,' Pete says.

I try to swallow, but my throat is full of stones. 'Is that why he died?' I ask.

Pete shrugs. 'When the cops came to search his room I whisked this out from under their noses.' His sudden grin betrays his pride at having outwitted the enemy. So far as I know, Pete has never been in trouble with the law, but it's clearly as important to him as it was to Max, to get the better of the police. 'I didn't know about the Filofax then,' he goes on. 'I found that later in my car. Fortunately the cops didn't think to look there. I buried this thing in the garden.'

I think of Ani and wonder if this is why she didn't want to talk to me about her brother. She advised me to get in touch with Pete if I wanted to know more. But there were things she

154

could have told me, I'm certain. I can't see her approving of the heroin. I can't see any of the family approving of that.

'Don't suppose you rescued Max's exercise books?' I ask.

'The ones he kept by his bed?'

'Yes.'

'Cops took those.'

'Thought so . . . Can I see the Filofax?' I ask, when we get back into the living room. At least this room doesn't look diseased. Untidy, sure — beer cans, ashtrays, newspapers, unwashed coffee cups — but it's much as it was when Max lived here. A large poster advertising an exhibition of young Maori artists hangs above the disused fireplace. I went to that exhibition with Max. It was one of our happy days.

A fit of coughing from the other end of the house warns that Sean might soon be joining us. 'Poor old bugger,' Pete comments.

'Why didn't Max borrow *your* car?' I ask, the Filofax momentarily forgotten.

'Eh?'

'The day before he died he asked to borrow mine. To go to your Auntie Petula's unveiling in the King Country.'

'He wasn't going there.'

'Are you sure?'

'I'm sure,' Pete says.

'Did any of you go?' I ask.

'Not to my knowledge.'

'Isn't that a bit odd?'

Pete shrugs.

'Max wrote me a story about his time in Ohura, when he lived there with his grandparents . . . Well, when your Nan died, Queenie didn't go to the tangi. No one from Auckland did. Can you explain that?'

Pete takes out his ventilator and plunges it into his mouth. His cheeks cave inwards as he takes in the deep, life-saving breaths. Ani advised me to question Queenie, not Pete, about Max's time at Ohura. But Pete must know something, surely.

'Look,' he says eventually, 'I wasn't around then. What would

155

I know? You'll have to ask Ela about it.'

'Sam Etuata,' I persist. 'It's to do with him, isn't it?'

'Ask Ela.'

'She's his daughter. She might not want to talk about him.'

'He was a bastard, I can tell you that.'

'Did he stop Queenie going to her mother's tangi?'

'Fancied himself as a matai.'

'So he did stop her . . .'

'Going on about his genealogy. Calling Mum *Maori scum*.'

'Did you ever meet him?'

'I'd have killed him if I had.'

I observe Pete anxiously. His struggle to breathe alarms me. I want to probe further, but fear the effect my inquiry is having. 'What happened to him?' I ask, hoping one last question will tell me what I want to know.

Pete throws his head back against the chair. 'Who knows?' he mutters. 'If there's any justice, which there ain't, he'd be doin' time. More likely he's swannin' round in Samoa someplace. Playin' the matai.'

I nod. It's beginning to make sense. A couple more questions and I might have the whole story. But I can't risk distressing Pete further.

'There was something going on between Mum and Auntie Petula,' Pete says, raising his head and firing the words at me as if anxious to be rid of them. 'Don't know what it was, but it was big. Us younger kids never met her of course, but we knew who she was. Mention her name, and you got a clip around the ear.'

'So they quarrelled . . .'

'More like they declared war.'

'And you've no idea what it was about?'

Pete's head slumps again. 'Look, Renate, don't push this, OK?' he pleads. 'Mum's not gunna like it if you do.'

I think of Will's words, and my promise to think the best of Queenie. Was she jealous of Auntie Petula because of Max's regard for her? Could it be something as simple as that? Somehow I don't think so. Queenie doesn't strike me as a jealous woman.

'Just leave it, OK?' Pete says again, running a nervous hand over his scalp.

Since I last saw Pete at Max's graveside he's shaved his head. It makes him look more monk-like than ever. 'Yeah, yeah, tell me about it!' I hear Max tease. 'You liked Pete with curls. Same way you liked me with hair hanging down my back. What is it with you and hair, Renate? Is it a sex thing?'

I try to imagine what Pete's life must be like now Max has gone. No job, a twenty-year-old car that keeps breaking down, no sign of a girlfriend, the ever-present threat of a fatal asthma attack.

'Is this a good time for me to look at the Filofax?' I suggest gently.

Pete nods and hoists himself up from his chair.

He's only just left the room when the front door opens and Alan walks in. We greet each other warmly. I tell him there's some tucker in the kitchen — pies and biscuits and fruit. I don't tell him about the beer.

'I've been thinkin',' Pete announces on his return. He glances at the kitchen from where Alan can be heard clattering crockery. 'That stuff we were talkin' about . . .'

'Yes?' I encourage. I have no idea what's coming. Is Pete referring to Sam Etuata? Or are we back with drugs? I've already pieced together an explanation of Max's death. The drugs belong with Pete's other revelation — Max's taste for gambling. Now, in the wake of the news that Max was involved with drugs, I begin to have an even clearer sense of the trouble he might have got into. That he would have incurred debts seems not just possible, but highly probable. How would he pay them? He could have gone back to the gang (*once you're a patched member you're marked for life*), but that wasn't Max's way any more. He would have chosen another route, one he felt he could navigate on his own. I'm not convinced he was *using* heroin — I'm sure I would have noticed the needle marks — but I'm prepared to concede he might have been selling it.

'It's about Paea,' Pete says, sitting in the collapsed armchair

Max always reckoned had his name carved on it. Like the arm-chair his grandfather sat in.

Again I nod. Paea, twin brother of Ela, son of Sam Etuata, was another person Max never talked about. The one time I questioned him he fobbed me off by saying he didn't really know him. At the time I accepted this explanation, though it later struck me as odd, since he knew Ela and Vincent, Sam's other son.

'I guess Max never said much about him,' Pete says.

'Not a word,' I answer. 'Clammed up, same as when I asked about Sam.'

'That would figure.'

'I thought I might get some answers from Ani. But she was as much of a closed book as Max.'

'Ani's no use. She's got other things on her mind.'

'She told me your mother married Sam after Max left.'

'Yeah.'

'Seems odd. Waiting till Max has gone to . . .'

'Not really,' Pete interrupts. 'Mum likes to be married.'

I become aware that my mouth has gone dry and glance at the kitchen. I'm beginning to regret not opening those beers.

'Thing is,' Pete says. 'Paea's got himself into a heap of trouble . . . Seems he's been . . . oh shit, Renate, why am I always the one to pass on the bad news?'

'Someone has to,' I joke, though neither of us is smiling.

'Paea has a problem. To do with kids. He likes to fuck them.'

I open my mouth, but I can't get any words past my throat. It's not so much that the information has shocked me, it's that I'm hearing it about Max's brother, not his stepfather. Because that, I realise now, is the answer I've been groping towards — Max was abused by his stepfather. It's the one thing that makes sense of everything else: Max's exile in Ohura; the estrange-ment from Queenie; his adoption by the gang. Queenie sent her son to live in Ohura for his own safety. But she had other reasons too. With Max gone she could marry Sam Etuata with-out feeling she was endangering her child. Perhaps she believed, as I once did, that there is magic in marriage. Perhaps she hoped to save two people by marrying — her son and his abuser.

'Paea was caught interfering with Bethany,' Pete goes on, his words prefaced by a deep, rasping intake of breath. 'It was a couple of years back now. Someone should have told you.'

'Jesus Christ! Did Max know?'

'What's that got to do with it?'

'*He'd* have told me,' I assert, though of course that's not true. Chances are, Max would have said nothing at all.

'Bethany's all right, Renate. No real harm done.'

'But you let Paea . . . You did nothing about it.'

'Not our way,' Pete says.

'What *is* your way then? Tell me.' I can't keep the anger out of my voice. I'm not even sure I want to. 'Bethany would have been, what? Eight years old?' I hiss at him. 'Max was six when . . . I'm right, aren't I?' I accuse. 'Paea, Sam, they were . . . are . . . both . . .'

'No harm done,' Pete repeats miserably.

'How can you say that when you know . . . I thought you wanted answers,' I remind him sharply.

'Lay off, Renate. Whatever happened to Max, and I'm not saying anything did, it was a long time ago and you can't blame . . . It's not an answer,' he finishes defiantly.

'That's easy to say,' I shoot back.

'Look, Mum told Paea to get the hell out. Live somewhere else. But she didn't call the cops, if that's what you're asking.'

'You know what riles me,' I mutter, 'you knew, all of you, and you never said . . .'

Pete gives me the opaque look. It's not unfriendly, not exactly, but it's definitely telling me to back off.

'You wanted to have a dekko at this,' he says, picking up the Filofax and handing it to me, as if we've been talking about nothing more controversial than the weather. 'Not that there's much to see,' he adds.

I glance at Alan, who's come into the room with a pie in one hand and a plate of biscuits in the other, and look down to see Max's name neatly printed on the imitation leather. When I open it, the first thing I see is a shopping list, with the price of each item recorded alongside. *Cigarette papers, matches, black wool, chocolate*, I read. On the opposite page is a list of books, presumably ones Max planned to read. Below that is a list of people, none of whose names I recognise. I realise Max can only have got this Filofax a week or two before he died. Pete was right. There's hardly anything in it.

Finally I turn to the diary section, and look up the date of his death. It's there all right, just as Vincent said. *Roy H 10 a.m.* And there's something else. An entry for the day before. *Income Support 3.15*. Underneath which Max has written, *No fucking change. No options left.*

I make a final check of the blank pages, and hand the Filofax back to Pete. 'You know what I'd like,' I say to him. 'I'd like to visit Max's grave again. Would you come with me?'

To my relief, Pete smiles. 'Any time, babe,' he answers. 'Just say the word.'

20

Over the next few weeks I brood, not on my new novel, but on
Pete's confesssion about Paea and that bleak entry in Max's
Filofax. *No options left.* I have no doubt those words are the key
to why he died. Income Support turned down whatever it was
he was applying for, leaving him only one place, or rather one
person, to turn to — Roy Harawira.

My dilemma is, should I go to the police with what I know?
I'm a white, middle-class, middle-aged female. It doesn't take
an Einstein to work out I'm more likely to be listened to than
Pete or Queenie. But the more I think about confiding in the
people Max regarded as the *enemy*, the more reluctant I become.
Better, at least initially, to confide in my mother. I've been de-
bating whether to send her Max's stories. Why not phone her to
say they're on their way, then tell her about my conversation
with Pete?

'I'm worried, darling,' she says, when my monologue is
ended. 'This Roy person. I have to say I don't like the sound of
him. Are you sure you're not getting in over your head?'

'I haven't done anything illegal, Mum,' I say.

'Withholding information?'

'It's not mine to withhold.'

I sense my mother smiling sceptically at the other end of the
phone, but what she says is straightforward enough. 'You must
definitely send me Max's stories.'

The following day, putting (with some reservations) Max's
exercise books into the post, I decide the person I need to talk to

is Ani. But it turns out she's down in Wellington, presenting a petition. The irritation I feel is illogical. Ani isn't being *deliberately* evasive.

My next move is to phone Queenie. I plan to ask her if she's heard anything from the coroner, though what I really want to talk to her about is Paea and Roy Harawira. To my surprise, I get through first time. The reason for that is soon made clear. Vincent and Gloria have moved out; and Lily, whose husband has been laid off, is spending all her time at her own place. Queenie tells me the house feels deserted.

Listening to her litany of complaint, I decide this is not the moment to ask questions. 'You never come an' see me,' Queenie accuses. 'You're as bad as the others.' My promise to visit at the weekend elicits a sceptical snort. 'See you when I see you,' she says.

The day Ani's due back my mother phones me. I assume she's ringing to talk about Max's stories ('very interesting, dear, very illuminating') but it seems she has more pressing things on her mind. 'Have you read this morning's paper?' she asks.

I start to remind her I don't read newspapers, but she interrupts me. 'You must look at the crime page,' she instructs.

I try to get her to tell me more, but all she'll say is, 'It concerns Max, but it shouldn't upset you too much. For once they haven't published every lurid detail. We'll talk about his stories later,' she promises.

I push the manuscript I'd been working on to the back of my desk, grab my purse and run down the road to the dairy. The front page of the *Herald* carries a picture of President Clinton, whose extramarital activities are apparently the most important thing going on in the world right now. I turn to the crime page. The first thing I see is Roy Harawira's name. It jumps out at me the way the letter Z, with its reminder of New Zealand, used to flash at me from the pages of British newspapers.

I read the article carefully. No temptation to skim read this time. *Police yesterday arrested a man in connection with a drug ring operating in a number of South Auckland secondary schools. The man,*

Roy Harawira, has been remanded in custody. It's believed Harawira is
the man police have been searching for in connection with a fatal accident
on the southern motorway at the end of last March.

Detective Filluel, who has been leading the investigation into the
schools' drug ring, described the arrest as a breakthrough. 'My team have
been working round the clock. We expect to make further arrests over the
next few weeks.

I put the paper down. My mother was wrong. I *am* upset.
She couldn't have known — it's not something Max writes about
in his stories — of his plan to train as a youth drug counsellor,
but *I* know. And now I'm being asked to believe that not only
did he turn his back on that vision, he actively betrayed it by
selling drugs to children.

The phone rings, but I ignore it. If, as I suspect, it's my
mother, I need to be in a calmer state before speaking to her. I
can guess why she wanted me to read the article. It lets me off
the hook for one thing. The police obviously know a great deal
more about Roy Harawira than I do. No need for me to add my
two cents worth. But my mother's main motive would have
been to do with Max. His name wasn't mentioned. Mum would
have wanted me to see it as a sign that the world was beginning
to lose interest in Maxwell Arapata Nene.

In the end I phone Mum myself. By that time I've talked to
Ani and arranged to go for a walk with her on Saturday. I don't
tell Mum about Max's failed plan. She's already decided he was
up to no good when he died. Instead we talk about the stories. 'I
see what you mean about him,' she says. 'There's an innocence
there, isn't there? Even when he's describing terrible things.'

'I knew you'd understand.'

'But they *are* terrible things, Renate. You should never forget
that.'

'I don't.'

'It seems to me, to be born as Max was, into a de-tribalised
family, with the added complication of a father and a stepfather
from different cultures, well, I've been trying to imagine it, and
I think it has to be a recipe for schizophrenia. I don't mean the

mental illness, but something every bit as bad — a handicap of monumental proportions. Cultural schizophrenia, I suppose you'd call it.'

'Max always swore he could handle it. Our world. The Maori world. He convinced me he had it all under control.'

'He was a good liar, Renate. You said so yourself.'

'*We* don't have to live in *his* world though. That's the difference, isn't it? He *has* to live in ours if he's to survive.'

My mother is silent for a moment. Then she says, 'You did your best, darling. You loved him.'

For the rest of the day I wrestle with competing sorrows: Max; Greg; the years when I failed to reach out to my mother; Cecil. But it's Max I keep returning to. I long to talk to him, to hear him tell me he wasn't selling drugs to schoolchildren, that there's another explanation. I conjure him up, but though I feel his presence, I neither see nor hear him.

With the approach of darkness my thoughts begin to form a pattern, at the centre of which stands Cecil. I know what he would say to me if he was here. That it isn't finished yet. That there's something more I have to do. 'But I'm tired,' I answer him. 'It's too hard on my own.'

'You're not tired,' he contradicts. 'You're afraid of what you might find.'

Two days later I meet Ani at the foot of Mount Eden. She's wearing a black anorak, blue jeans and a green baseball cap. She looks like a model on a day off.

We both comment on the unseasonal warmth. 'End of July. Isn't that supposed to be winter?' I remark tritely.

As we walk towards the path that will take us to the summit, I ask Ani about her trip to Wellington. She's reluctant to go into detail. All she'll tell me is that petitions on behalf of urban Maori were presented to the Ministers of Education and Maori Development. 'You can read about it in the papers,' she says.

I tell her I'd rather hear it from her, but she dismisses my words with an eloquent gesture. 'What you have to understand,

Renate,' she says, 'is that democracy's no use to Maori. It's not how we did things in the past, and it's not how we do things now.'

'So why bother with petitions?'

This time there's no gesture, just the opaque look.

We pick our way across the cattle-stop dividing the road from the mountain and start the climb to the summit. I've been careful to refer to the mountain by its Maori name, Maungawhau, the Hill of the Whau Plant. What I didn't know, but Ani tells me as we puff our way upwards, is that the flower of the whau plant was used by the early settlers as a soap. 'So it's really the Hill of the Soap Plant,' she explains, laughing.

I'm relieved at the change in her mood. Perhaps she'll tell me one of her risqué jokes. Or was that another thing Max made up?

We don't say much more till we reach the top. Then, having disposed of the usual superlatives about the view — Maungawhau is the highest of Auckland's cluster of volcanoes, with a panoramic view of the city and its twin harbours — we select a bench and sit down.

'Before you tell me what you wanted to see me about,' Ani says, 'there's something I should tell you.'

I try not to look surprised. Ani isn't one to volunteer information. Is she going to tell me about the petitions after all?

'Last time we talked you asked me why Mum didn't go to my grandmother's tangi.'

My mouth drops open in astonishment. This was one of the things I'd planned to question her about. Is she a mind-reader, as well as everything else?

'She couldn't,' Ani continues. 'The twins were in hospital.'

'I see . . .'

'I don't think you do.'

'Then you better explain,' I suggest tersely.

'Sam Etuata put them there,' Ani says.

'In hospital?'

'He was a violent man.'

I stare at the city spread at my feet like a gift. Does Ani know how hard I've been searching for this information? Is she going to be the person who completes the jigsaw for me? 'My understanding,' I say softly, 'is he was more than that. Worse, I mean.'

Ani touches her lips as if to warn me, in this deserted place, of eavesdroppers. 'That's my understanding too,' she murmurs.

'So he didn't just *hit* his children . . .'

'I can't answer that, Renate. You'd have to ask them. But I'm ninety per cent sure he abused Max.'

'Yes,' I agree, adding, 'I'm sorry. This must be hard for you.'

'Nothing new about hard,' Ani says, flashing me a sardonic smile.

'It makes an awful kind of sense,' I admit. 'Things Max said. Things Pete told me.'

'Am I supposed to be glad about that?'

'Don't you want to know why Max . . .'

'Not particularly. What purpose does it serve? It won't bring him back.'

'No,' I concede. 'But it might help . . .'

'Why can't you just accept that he's gone?'

I think about answering, but change my mind. The thought of accepting without knowing depresses me.

'This need to know, to find explanations, it's a Pakeha thing, isn't it? Where I'm coming from, there are a whole different set of questions.'

'Yes, well,' I start to say, but the words of protest die on my lips. I suspect Ani enjoys creating mysteries she has no intention of solving. 'Why didn't you tell me about Sam Etuata before?' I ask.

'Because I wasn't sure of you.'

'And now you are?'

This time Ani's smile lingers. 'You'll do,' she says.

I savour the words for a moment. Then, encouraged by them, I bring up the subject of Queenie's relationship with Auntie Petula, another question I came here to ask. 'Pete thought there'd been a quarrel,' I confide. 'I figured it must have had something to do with why none of you went to her tangi.'

'I didn't go because I couldn't,' Ani anwers brusquely. 'I was needed elsewhere. I can't speak for the others.'

'And your grandfather, when he died . . .'

'You'd have to ask Mum about that.'

I pull a wry face. 'Somehow I don't think Queenie would appreciate . . .'

'Why is all this so important to you?' Ani interrupts. 'I thought it was Max's motives you were trying to fathom, not Mum's.'

'It's all connected, isn't it?'

'If you say so.'

'You think I'm interfering?'

'I think you're losing sight of the bigger picture.'

'What's that supposed to mean?'

Ani removes her cap, twirls it in her hand, then jams it back on her head. 'If you want to know what I think,' she volunteers, 'I think my mother and Auntie Petula quarrelled over Sam Etuata. From the little I know of our venerable great-aunt, I don't think she'd have minced words. She'd have told Mum to chuck Sam out and start taking proper care of her children.'

I nod. Something in Ani's manner tells me the subject is now closed.

For a few moments we sit in silence, staring at the view. Does Ani know about Paea, I wonder? Of course she does, I decide, glancing at her. But I can guess what she'd say if I brought his name into our conversation. 'What is it with you, Renate? This need of yours to dot every *i* and cross every *t*, is it a Pakeha thing? Get over it! Move on.'

'Do you believe the dead come back?' I ask, when I judge the silence has gone on long enough. Of all the questions I came here to ask, this is the one I've been most nervous about.

Ani fixes her amazing eyes on me. I'm not sure how to interpret her expression, but I *think* it's sympathetic. 'In our culture the dead are never far away,' she says. 'I think it's harder for you Pakeha.'

'I read somewhere that the dead come back to us through

fiction. That they help us carry the burdens we couldn't otherwise manage. But I'm not talking about fiction . . .'

Ani plaits her fingers together, then turns her hands round so the fingers become the pews in a church. Is the gesture deliberate I wonder? A Pakeha puzzle acted out for my benefit? 'What's important about the dead,' she says, 'is what they're trying to tell you. Usually their job is to take you back to your roots, to remind you that what lies in the past can be healing. Hope, you see, isn't just a future thing. Hoping *for* something. Hoping to get something. That's how it operates in your culture. For Maori it has as much to do with the past as with the future. That's why we've stayed strong.'

'I've seen Max, Ani. I've talked to him. I didn't imagine it.'

'Of course you didn't.'

Her tone is so matter-of-fact I can't help smiling. The grin she gives me in response briefly conjures up her brothers.

'You see those terraces,' she says, pointing down the hill. 'Back in the eighteenth century this was a very important pa. The Waiohau tribe owned most of what is now Auckland. Then the Ngapuhi invaded and the Waiohau lost their lands.'

'Max was Ngapuhi, wasn't he?'

'Through his father, yes.'

'Ani . . .'

She turns to me. I've not seen that particular expression on her face before. I realise she has something important to tell me. 'My father was Rongowhakaata,' she announces. 'The tribe of Te Kooti.'

I know that's not all she has to say, so I nod, and wait. In my German great-grandmother's day Te Kooti was a name used to frighten children: just as 'Boney' once struck fear into the hearts of English children. The truth of course is a lot more complex. Te Kooti was a terrifying figure, to his own race as well as to the Pakeha, but he was also a visionary who led his people first in war against the settlers, then in an impassioned call for peace. 'There'll be no more wars by the Maori people with the Europeans,' he famously said. 'The last will be with me.'

And it was. Till now, I think, looking at Ani, whose eyes seem to be drilling a hole in my skull.

'Are you familar with the prophecy?' Ani asks me.

I shake my head.

'He talked of the One who would come after him.'

'A regular John the Baptist,' I murmur.

Ani smiles. 'He knew his scriptures,' she agrees.

The smile disarms me. Perhaps I imagined that penetrating look? This is *history* we're discussing, I remind myself, not the present.

'The One who finds his bones will be the One who completes his task,' Ani says.

'That shouldn't be too difficult. Finding his bones, I mean.'

'On the contrary. No one knows where his grave is. The body was moved.'

I look down at the terraced hillside, seeing for a moment the terrible battle that took place there, imagining Max amongst the invading forces. That he would have made a fearless warrior is something I've never doubted.

If I were to ask Ani what Te Kooti's task was, or rather is, since it hasn't been completed yet, would she tell me? I glance at her, but her face is turned away.

'Ha! haere mai, e nga iwi o te motu,

Hari-a mai, te pouri nui . . .'

The words, chanted at Max's burial, repeat themselves in my head. If I close my eyes I can see the men, Max's friends, several of them on day release from Pare, stamping their feet, waving their arms in sorrowful welcome, their voices rising above the wails of the womenfolk, as his coffin approached its final resting place.

'The people will never see me again,' Ani says, still with her face averted. 'But the land will see me.'

'Te Kooti's words?' I guess.

She nods.

'You've found the bones, haven't you?' I whisper. 'You're the One he talked about.'

169

The suggestion is greeted with a hoot of laughter. I'm so taken aback, I laugh too. 'No wonder Max liked you,' Ani says.

'He told me you were a kuia,' I confess, feeling a need to explain. 'He said you were too young, but that's what you were all the same.'

'Did he now?'

'He said you had a vision. Like Te Kooti.'

'Ah . . .' Ani says.

'Look, I don't mean to pry, and you can tell me to shut up if you want, but I know you're involved in something, not just the usual protests, but . . .'

I didn't imagine those penetrating eyes. I can feel them boring into me again. 'Go on,' Ani encourages.

'Was Max involved too?' I blurt out. 'Was that the reason he died?'

Waiting for her to answer I hear the chant again, see the blurred faces of the mourners following the coffin up the bank.

'I'm sorry, Renate,' Ani says at last. 'I'd like to be able to tell you he died for the cause, but it wouldn't be true. It isn't even true that there is a cause. Not in the way you mean.'

'So why tell me all that stuff about Te Kooti?' I challenge.

Ani presses her lips together. I prepare myself for another long wait, but she answers quickly. 'There's something you should know,' she says. 'I didn't trust Max. I don't have your generosity of spirit, I'm afraid. I'm not saying we didn't have things in common, things we could talk about, but it only went so far. I wish I could tell you different, Renate, I really do. Pete told me about the heroin. I know what you must be thinking.'

Our eyes meet. In hers is an unmistakable expression of sympathy — as if my continuing to think the best of Max made her feel sorry for me.

'The coroner's report should shed some light,' she says.

She means to be kind, I know, but her words depress me. 'Does it have to be this way?' I whisper. 'Can *you* tell me?'

'What way?'

'Divided. You, me. Maori, Pakeha. Police, gangs. Them, us.

Why, Ani?'

Her answer is unhesitating. 'Power,' she says. 'You took ours when you took our land. Now we want it back.'

That night Max appears at the foot of my bed, just as he did in my dream after the tangi. I stare at him. He smiles back. I wait for him to speak. 'Thank you, Renate,' he says, in his almost inaudible voice.

'For what?' I ask.

'We're both getting sorted now,' he says.

21

Blessed is he whose transgression is forgiven, whose sin is covered . . .

I'm sitting in Queenie's overheated lounge, staring at Max's handwriting. Yesterday, while Ani and I were walking on the Hill of the Soap Plant, the police returned Max's belongings to Queenie. Nobody knows whether everything was returned or not. Nobody thought to ask. 'There were two of them,' Queenie explained when I arrived. 'A big bloke, tall as the doorway. And a policewoman, a Maori.'

'And you didn't ask to see the list?'

'What list?'

'They have to list every item they take. Isn't that right?' I look to Will for help, but he merely shrugs.

'Why would they take his shoes?' Ela wants to know. 'They took his shoes,' she informs me, unnecessarily.

'They'd have taken his soul if they could find it,' Queenie answers her daughter.

It's Sunday. I can hear church bells ringing in the distance. The priest who officiated at Max's tangi was a relative; a Tuwharetoa kaumatua. He was a Catholic, which surprised me. The church Max professed allegiance to was Anglican. But in the extraordinary atmosphere of those days of mourning, divisions, whether religious or tribal, far from distracting from the proceedings, seemed to enhance them. Max was Anglican; his siblings, in so far as they had a religion, were Ringatu, the faith founded by Te Kooti; Queenie was, or rather, had been, a Pentecostal. Yet everyone accepted Father Ralph and the rituals of

172

the Catholic Church, movingly mixed with Maori ceremony.

As if religion didn't provide complication enough, Max's tribal affiliations were so diverse, Father Ralph joked that he was probably related to half the iwi in the North Island. The same went for his siblings, three of whom had the added distinction of being part Samoan. Attending the tangi were representatives from Ngapuhi, Tuhoe, his mother's Ngati Maniopoto and — under the leadership of Father Ralph — Tuwharetoa. It struck me as sad that so many people came to honour Max in death. Where were they when he was alive? And where was his father?

As for the Pakeha presence — I was by no means the only fair-skinned person there — that too might have been a source of conflict but, mercifully, was not. As one mourner after another approached Max's coffin, spoke or not according to protocol, put down their koha, then withdrew, it was as if we were united by an invisible, many-stranded thread. No one who came to that tangi could be described as rich. Many were obviously poor. Yet when the time came to gather up the koha, enough money had been donated to pay for several tangi. As for the other gifts — flowers, photos, items of clothing, mementos — they stayed in the coffin with Max. He would not go unaccompanied on his journey to the underworld.

Over those long, sorrowful days I grew accustomed to the signs of grief — the wailing, the sobbing, the dramatic orations — but nothing had prepared me for the sound that issued from Queenie's throat when, on the final day, the moment came to close the lid of the coffin. It was a sound from the centre of the earth; a cry so desolate it echoed long after the voice had been silenced. It took all Father Ralph's authority to persuade Queenie, and her equally distraught daughters, to let go of the coffin and allow Max's final journey to begin.

'Haere atu ra!' the old woman, who for three days had led every karanga, cried out, as the coffin was carried from the house. 'Haere atu ra!' Farewell.

Again and again those words were heard, as the slow procession made its way to the burial ground. I can hear them still,

173

falling on my ears with the same shrill persistence as the wailing of gulls.

'The books are yours,' Queenie announces, breaking into my reverie. 'Max would want you to have them.'

I jump up from the sofa, cross the room and throw my arms around her.

'You taught him to write,' Queenie says.

'I gave him the means, that's all,' I protest. 'He was a writer already.'

When I'm seated again, and can trust myself to speak, I tell Queenie that Max's books — there are two of them — both start with quotations from the Psalms. 'He was very keen on the Psalms,' I explain.

'Read it to me,' Queenie instructs.

I open the first book, the one with every page filled, and read out loud, 'Blessed is he whose transgression is forgiven, whose sin is covered . . .'

'I thought so,' Queenie interrupts.

I look at her enquiringly.

'It's the Psalm of Te Kooti,' she tells me.

I glance down the page. Max has written out the whole of the Psalm, but these words he's underlined, **Thou art my hiding place; thou shalt preserve me from trouble; thou shalt compass me about with songs of deliverance . . .**

My eyes fill with tears.

'You'll stay, won't you?' Queenie says. 'You won't rush off like you did last time?'

I glance round at the others, at Will who is smiling, and Ela who is looking bored, and the children who are playing a game of cards. 'I'd love to, Queenie,' I say. 'Thank you.'

That night we squash around the table in the kitchen and eat generous quantities of boiled pork and puha, accompanied by large chunks of Maori bread. Thanks to Walter, who turned up with his children in the late afternoon, we also have a plentiful supply of beer.

Walter's arrival was the signal for his eldest child, Rewi, the one who lives with Queenie, to demand money so he could go out with his mates. When I first got to know the family I assumed Rewi was the reason Walter spent so much time at his mother's house. But as with so many other things to do with Max and his whanau, I was wrong. It's customary for sons and daughters to hand over one of their children for the grandparents to raise. What Meriana, Walter's wife, makes of the arrangement I've no idea. Like her sister-in-law, Ani, Meriana is something of a 'ghost'. But I've seen no signs of distress in Rewi, a sturdy fourteen-year-old, with, judging by this afternoon's colourful exchange, a typically combative relationship with his father. As for Walter's other children, they treat Rewi in exactly the same way as they treat one another. The fact that he doesn't live with them is clearly irrelevant.

As we eat our pork and puha and drink the dark beer favoured by Walter, we talk of Max, and the ways in which he delighted, annoyed, enraged, enlightened and betrayed us. When we've exhausted the topic we talk of his father, a subject I'd imagined till now was taboo. Max, it seems, not only didn't know his father, he never set eyes on him. 'Bastard disappeared the day I told him I was pregnant,' Queenie explains. 'I was in the fourth form at Ohura School. He was working on the railways. Big handsome sod he was, with a cheesecake smile. Rickie Kunaiti. May God punish him for his sins.'

'Where is he now?' I ask. 'Does anyone know?'

'Last I heard he was running a fishing boat off Opunake,' Queenie says. 'He'd have found some woman down there with a bit of money. He's good at finding women with money. Mind you, that was several years ago. He's probably moved on by now.'

'So he wouldn't know about Max then?'

'He didn't want to know about him when he was born. Why should he want to know now he's dead?'

It's on the tip of my tongue to ask about Auntie Petula, but then I remember Pete and think better of it. Queenie, I'm beginning to realise, is something of a law unto herself. A tangi is traditionally a time of healing and reconciliation, but that doesn't seem to be how it works for Queenie. There was to be no reconciliation with Max's father; just as there was none, in the past, with Auntie Petula.

'So what happened to *you*?' I ask instead. (You wanted me to know these things, didn't you Max? I silently challenge. You set this evening up.) 'Did you have to leave school?'

Queenie laughs and takes out a cigarette. 'Followed the bastard, didn't I?' she confesses, leaning across the table to share in the match Ela has just struck. 'Hitched a ride to Auckland, more fool me. But the bugger was always one step ahead. Then I had my lucky break. Met Hemi, Rickie's cousin. He offered to help me find him. Not that we ever did,' she adds, giggling.

'Hemi?' I enquire, glancing round the table.

'My father,' Walter answers.

'And Ani's,' Queenie puts in.

'So you and Hemi . . .' I say, looking at Queenie.

'Best husband I ever had,' she tells me. 'Till I met Will, of course,' she adds, grinning across the table at husband number three.

'Get away with you,' Will responds, though it's obvious he's pleased.

'What happened to him?' I ask.

'He died.'

'I'm sorry.'

'I married him, then buried him,' Queenie says. 'It goes like that sometimes.'

'So he died when the children were young?'

'Walter doesn't remember him, do you boy?'

Walter gestures sadly.

'And you never saw Rickie Kunaiti again?'

'Heard about him from time to time. This woman, that woman. Up north for a bit. A spell in Tokoroa at the timber mill. A job on a farm near Marton. But I never saw him, no.'

While we talk the children run in and out; the television gets turned up, then down, but never off; the phone rings and Ela disappears for half an hour, returning to the table with flushed cheeks and shining eyes; Lily arrives with her children in tow; more chairs are pulled up; more food dished out; more beer poured. At one point I start to tell Queenie about my walk with Ani, but am silenced by a kick under the table from Will. Least I assume it's Will. Max, whose presence in this room is as real to me as the beer in my glass, could just as easily have been the one responsible.

At ten o'clock Queenie orders the grandchildren to bed. They, however, have other ideas. Seems they've been working on a waiata, which they insist on performing for us.

With much scraping of chairs and refilling of glasses we make our way from the kitchen to the living room, sitting down wherever we can. Bethany, the leader of the group, has already hauled a mattress off one of the beds and placed it along the far wall. That's where I sit, with Ela and Lily and the younger children, under the picture of the wharekura. Queenie goes back to her usual chair. Walter and Will sit on the sofa.

I find myself watching Bethany, admiring the skill with which she organises her cousins and siblings; conscious of the proud flush in her cheeks as she sets the stage for the waiata. 'No harm done,' Pete said. I hope to God he's right.

Giggling and nudging each other, the children eventually line themselves up in front of the television, which Bethany switches off, to my relief. There seems to be some doubt as to whether the waiata is to be introduced or not. Walter's second boy, Jimmy, clearly tired of being bossed about by a girl, announces to the assembled company that Bethany has something to say. He gets a whack across the back for his pains. This sets Lily's daughter, Greta, off on a wail of protest, provoking a second slap for Jimmy, this time from Ela's son, Albert. In the end Bethany sorts things out to everyone's satisfaction and, after a wobbly start, the waiata proceeds.

'Engari te titi e tangi haere ana, e
Whai tokorua rawa raua . . .'
I understand only some of the words, but the sweetness of

the singing needs no explaining. Max used to tease me for assuming all Maori were natural harmonisers. 'But they are,' I argue now, looking at his photo, partly visible behind the singers. 'Listen to your nieces and nephews.'

'And where did we learn to sing like that?' he argues back. 'You think we ran around the hills singing sentimental love songs in three-part harmony? We copied *your* people, Renate. We were good learners.'

'But you're better at it than we are,' I point out.

'Exactly,' Max agrees.

Is it an illusion, or is the photo grinning at me?

The song ends to enthusiastic applause and a request from Queenie for an encore. But the group only have the one offering, so they sing it again, while Queenie wipes away tears, and Lily, leaning over to me, explains in a whisper that this was Max's favourite waiata.

Another thing I didn't know about him.

Later Bethany tells me what the words mean. 'Even the titi as it goes, crying, travels in a pair . . .'

I have to turn away so she won't see my face. Self-pity has momentarily overwhelmed me. I stare at the door, not in the hope of seeing Max, but in the even more absurd hope of seeing Greg. How could I have lost him? Where did it go wrong? Our marriage was meant to be forever.

'Oh bird!' Bethany continues, 'I am like the kiwi egg abandoned on the beech tree. The roots grow over it. When the mother returns for the hatching the offspring are trapped, like me.'

'No wonder it sounded so sad,' I remark.

'Everyone's sad, aren't they?' Bethany answers. '*You* are.'

'Not always,' I protest.

'My dad is,' Bethany confides. 'He misses my mum.'

'Yes, well, *you* shouldn't be sad,' I insist, primly. 'You're young.'

The party doesn't break up till after midnight. The room is a mess, but it's agreed we'll clean up in the morning. Queenie, when I go to kiss her goodnight, calls me tamahine, daughter.

I cling to her wordlessly.

I'm to share a room with Ela and her two youngest, both of whom, thankfully, are asleep. I feel guilty wishing I could have a room to myself. It's not Ela or the babies I object to, it's because I want to read Max's books. They are beginning to take on the aura of holy relics.

While Ela's in the bathroom I sneak a look at the opening pages. Te Kooti's Psalm is followed by some words which I take to be Te Kooti's own. **Then we will all know that that is the day of the Prophecies . . . on which we will come together to be one in our direction and our canoe.**

There's no date on the cover of the book, or on any of the subsequent pages, so I've no way of knowing when Max wrote those words. Was Ani speaking the truth when she said he wasn't involved in the cause? Or non-cause, as she insists on describing it. I'm assuming Te Kooti is *her* ancestor, not Max's. So if what she said is true, Max's interest in Te Kooti, evidenced in these pages, is no more than a coincidence.

'Ela,' I say, when we're both in bed, a bed we have to share not just with each other, but with Queenie's evil-smelling Rottweilers. ('They always sleep in here,' Ela explained earlier. 'It was Mum's idea. She reckons I need guarding. Like, I'm supposed to be a magnet for every rapist in Auckland! What kind of a mother thinks like that, for Christ's sake?') 'Does Te Kooti have a special significance for you?' I ask. 'I'm wondering, you see, why Max quotes him so much.'

'Te Kooti, Te Shmooti,' Ela answers. 'Can't be bothered with all that stuff.'

'You think of yourself as Samoan?'

'Give us a break!'

'What then?'

'I think of myself as Ela Yakich. Well, maybe not any more. Ela Etuata? Nah. Don't wanna go back to that. Maybe I should just call myself Ela. Like that model. What's her name? Elle.'

'She does have a surname.'

'Yeah I know, Elle MacPherson. But she's Elle to most people, isn't she?'

'Do you remember much about your father?'

'Enough to want to forget him.'

'What was he like?'

'A booze artist. Booze for breakfast, booze for lunch, booze for tea. What else d'you wanna know?'

'Did he ever abuse you?' are the words on my lips. But I don't say them. Does this mean I've started to move on?

I wriggle my feet out from under one of the dogs. Ela yawns. 'Everyone knows about Te Kooti,' she says. 'He's one of those blokes, isn't he? Hone Heke, Te Rauparaha, Rewi Maniopoto, Te Kooti . . . Losers, if you want my opinion. Just like that useless bunch we had in parliament.'

I grin at her in the darkness. 'You sound just like your brother,' I say.

'Max? He was a loser too.'

22

Does any person know who his father is?

I stare at Max's handwriting in disbelief. I never knew he'd read *The Odyssey*. Yet here he is, in page after page, searching for the meaning of Odysseus' ten-year exile; returning again and again to the separation from family, to the journey into the underworld, to the terrible, life-threatening ordeals. Some of his comments are in Maori, but enough is in English for me to get the gist.

Like Odysseus, Max was on a search. Judging from his comments he saw himself most often as the lost son, but clearly there were moments when he identified with the father. Was it the living father he was searching for? The philandering Rickie Kunaiti? Or was it the father of myth, the buried father in himself? And if that was the case, who was the son? Was he a mythical figure too? Or could Max have repeated his father's pattern and had a child none of us know about? Anything, I realise, as I struggle to unravel the web of his thoughts, is possible.

What strikes me, as I turn the pages covered with Max's uneven handwriting, is that this process of unravelling is like unpicking knitting. Could this be why Max chose knitting as a hobby? Making a pattern from disparate threads gave him a sense of control . . . It feels like, if not an answer, then at least an explanation as to why I'm sitting here, in my flat, pulling the pattern of Max's thoughts to pieces.

Perhaps the answer as to whether Max had a child or not was there in front of me, at the tangi? The girl who wept so much

181

could have been pregnant. Though that theory doesn't really hold up either. Surely if she'd been pregnant, she would have told someone. Queenie would have welcomed a child of Max's as if it were a gift from God.

Near the end of his long meditation on Odysseus Max has written these words, they aren't in quote marks, but I assume them to be a precis of something he was reading. **The Greek word for good is agathos, for bad, kathos. But it's not the same as the Christian idea of good and evil. For Christians, good is seen as overcoming evil. That's the meaning of the Resurrection. For the Greeks, agathos and kathos were seen as eternally connected. The light and the dark were aspects of the whole, so human beings, rather than trying to overcome dark with light, had to make their peace with both.**

Compared to some of his later ramblings, this strikes me as impressively lucid.

The fascists who run this country are no different from men like Duke who run gangs, he's written elsewhere. **Intimidation. That's their weapon. 'If you don't do what we want we'll close your fucking town down.' For town, read factory or school or whatever. Power. That's what it's about. Ani's right. Power is where it's at.**

Once again I wonder about Ani. I haven't seen anything in the papers about her petitions. Was she trying to put me off the scent? Or was she testing me in some way? Seeing if I would take her words on trust.

Scattered in the margins of Max's writings are doodlings of various kinds — tattoos; stick figures; graffitti-style lettering. One of the more fleshed-out figures wears an All Black jersey and has his hand raised in a Black Power salute. But what stands out for me are the words Max quotes from the Bible. Dotted randomly through the text, they appear to follow a pattern of sorts. Most of the quotes are from the Psalms, but a verse from Isaiah brings a lump to my throat. **He hath sent me to bind up the broken-hearted, to proclaim liberty to the captives, and the opening of the prison to them that are bound.**

Sometimes what he's written makes no sense at all. There are lists of rhymes, **fuck muck buck duck**, and poems (I assume they're poems) where the word 'black' occurs on every line. Black and dark seem to be his favourite adjectives. Towards the end of the second book they occur on almost every line.

Maori shouldn't live as if their deprivations are privileges. Now where did that come from? It doesn't sound like Ani. **Glorying in our victim status is a pain in the bum.** I can sense him grinning when he writes like that. **Living within a formula of the oppressed — that sucks!** Not just grinning, laughing.

But Max's humour, intermittent in the first book, disappears altogether from the second. After nearly two hours of unravelling, dismayed by the increasing incoherence of his thoughts (was he on heroin when he wrote the final pages?) I get up, draw the curtains and make myself a cup of coffee. I try to tell myself Max's confusions were no worse than anyone else's, but I know that's not true. Wallace Stevens wrote, *The way through the world is more difficult to find than the way beyond it.* Stevens was Cecil's favourite poet. He used to read him to me in the cottage in Cornwall. I will always associate his lines with the plaintive crying of gulls. 'It's not finished, Renate. It won't be finished until . . .'

'Until what, Cecil? Until I'm beyond the world, like you?'

Next morning I phone Lily. She listens to what I have to say, but isn't able to shed any light. What she does say, is that if Max had a child, or was going to have a child, she would have known about it. 'You can't hide a thing like that,' she insists. 'Anyway, why would he want to? Mum would have loved another mokopuna.'

'That's what I thought,' I agree.

When I ask her if she knew anything at all about the girl at the tangi, she reaffirms what I'd already been told — no one knew who she was or where she came from. 'Probably someone Max picked up,' she says.

'Did he make a habit of doing that?'

'He always had a woman, Renate. He couldn't manage

without one. Surely you knew that?'

No I didn't, I silently reply. It wasn't the impression he gave *me* at all.

The next person I phone is Pete. He can't shed any light on the girl, but he's more prepared than before to talk about Paea. He even opens up about Sam Etuata. 'He was a hard man,' he tells me. 'I don't think he . . . you know . . . not his own kids. But he did take to them with his fists. Landed them in hospital a few times.'

'Why did Queenie put up with it?' I ask.

'Why does any woman?' Pete replies.

Paea, Pete tells me, has been refused bail. There was a hearing yesterday in Hamilton. The trial is set for October. Queenie has been told. Her reaction was much as Pete had anticipated. Sorrow rather than anger. But she'll support her son at his trial. Pete had anticipated that too. 'Our mother, she's our bones,' he explains.

But she wasn't Max's bones, I want to argue. If she had been, she'd have looked after him better, not sent him away. She'd have visited him in prison. Or is that not how it was? Just how Max wanted me to think it was.

'Will you go with Queenie?' I ask Pete.

'Yep,' he answers. 'We'll all go. Will. Vincent, if he hasn't found a job. Walter . . .'

Max would have gone too, if he'd been here.

The last thing Pete and I talk about is our proposed visit to Max's grave. We arrange to go the following weekend. 'Kia ora!' Pete says, as our conversation ends. 'You be good now.'

I go back to my work, determined to put questions about Max out of my mind. Twenty minutes later all I have to show is one rewritten sentence.

The warm weather has continued, confusing winter with spring. It's not just tui that wake me in the mornings now, but tits and finches and waxeyes. The jasmine is producing blossom a month early. So is the kowhai in the next-door garden. Everywhere I look I see Nature busy about its eternal business. Is that why I can't work? April is the cruellest month . . .

Three days pass. I talk to my mother, an unsatisfactory conversation which leaves me feeling guilty. I know what she wants. She wants me to 'move on' from Max, to let him rest in peace. But she doesn't understand. He's not sorted yet, and neither am I.

In an attempt to cheer myself up I ring Tess and arrange to meet in a café the following day. In addition to being a biographer, Tess also writes a weekly column for *The Herald*. Without actually articulating what I want to talk to her about, I find myself thinking back to the report of Roy Harawira's arrest, and wondering if there's any way of counteracting the inference that Max was involved in selling drugs to schoolchildren. Tess and I have talked many times about Max's crimes. At first it was hard for her to accept my affection for Max was genuine; but once she'd met him her attitude changed. And being Tess, she didn't just leave it there. She began looking into our sentencing record in this country, and asking in her *Herald* column, and elsewhere, why Maori almost invariably get longer sentences than their Pakeha counterparts. And why, since the system was clearly not working — recidivism figures are high — something wasn't being done to bring this cycle of hopelessness to an end?

But our meeting is not a success. It's my fault. The things I want to talk to her about come out in a jumble, and I can see that all I'm doing is worrying her again. We talk about my visit to Queenie and I give her a garbled account of Max's writings, but all the time I keep hearing my mother's voice, and mixing it up with Tess'. Even when the focus shifts and we start talking about Tess' current project, my mother's gentle warnings intrude. 'You must be sick to death of my muddles,' I say to her, as we're leaving.

'I wish you'd tell me what's really on your mind,' she answers me.

Driving away from the café I find myself on the waterfront road, heading, not for my flat in Mt Albert, but for Greg's house in St Heliers. I don't know why I'm doing this, but as I pull up outside the house I start to laugh. What was I hoping to achieve? A glimpse of Greg and Maggie living in domestic bliss?

'This isn't healthy,' I hear Max say. 'You shouldn't be doing this.'

'Then tell me what the hell I should be doing,' I snap back at him.

I arrive home to a flashing answerphone and a sense of loneliness so acute I dissolve into self-pitying tears. 'That's better,' Max soothes. 'No shame in tears.'

'I thought shame was what killed you,' I remind him sulkily.

I glare at his photo in the montage above my desk. This time there is no doubt. Max is grinning at me.

'I don't want your humour,' I hiss at him. 'I want answers.'

'Then go find them,' he instructs.

The answer is so typical of Max in his know-it-all mood I can't help laughing. I suppose he thinks *he's* helping *me* now.

I pick myself up from the chair into which I'd collapsed and walk over to the desk. The first message is from Tess. 'Darling, I'm worried about you,' she says. 'You were like a jack-in-the box today. And I'm not sick of hearing about Max, if that's what was bugging you. I want to help, for Christ's sake!'

I murmur 'sorry' into the receiver and resolve to phone her as soon as I've listened to the rest of my messages.

Something happens then which, though irrational (sceptics would say impossible), is all of a piece with what's been going on for me since Max died. It's triggered by the next message on my answerphone. It's from my English friend Daphne, wife of Cecil's partner, Robert. As I listen to her voice, my heart starts to beat a polka in my chest. Daphne wants to come and see me. She's been invited to a family wedding in Sydney and wonders how I would feel about her coming on to visit me.

I play the message again; rehearsing what I will say in reply; images from the past swimming in my head, as I listen to her voice, forgotten till this moment, but suddenly familiar again.

I glance at my watch — too early to phone back, Daphne will be asleep. Why am I so affected by the thought of seeing her again? Why is my heart beating like this?

The answer comes quickly, and from an unexpected quarter. 'England isn't finished for you,' a male voice declares.

It's not Cecil, not this time, but my British publisher, Brian Hannah, a man I haven't thought about in over a year. Since returning to New Zealand I've published two novels and a collection of short stories. I offered them to Brian, but he turned them down. So why am I conjuring him up now? It can't be anything to do with the abandoned novel. He wouldn't have liked that any more than the ones he rejected.

'No, but I like the one you haven't written yet,' his voice tolls in my head. 'The one called *Loving Max*.'

I jump up from the desk, open a bottle of wine, and pour myself a drink. I am gripped by an irrational conviction that the novel will be written, Brian will publish it and my life will start again. 'You're behind this, Max, aren't you?' I say out loud.

I walk over to his photo and touch the markings on his face. I may not have found what I was looking for, but the question I haven't dared ask for the last two years, about what I'm going to do with the rest of my life, has been answered. 'Thank you,' I whisper.

'Don't mention it,' Max whispers back.

I finish the wine in my glass, pick up the phone, call Tess and apologise for being so obtuse this afternoon. I tell her it's all to do with my mother and she laughs. I also tell her about Daphne, but decide to keep the rest to myself. The time to talk about the novel is when I've started writing it.

The rest of the messages are easily dealt with; until I get to the last one. It's from Queenie. 'We heard from the coroner's office today,' she announces, her voice thick with the importance of what she is communicating. 'The report will be delivered in the morning.'

I play the message again to be sure I've heard it right; then I dial Queenie's number. 'What happens now?' I ask Will, when the phone is eventually answered.

'We go to court,' he tells me. 'Ten o'clock, coroner's court in

187

Manurewa. Can you be there?'

'Of course,' I assure him.

'Queenie sends her love.'

'Hug her for me, Will,' I instruct.

'Sure thing.'

'Are you a praying man?'

There's a pause. I think I hear him scratching. Then he says, 'Might give it a go tonight. How about you?'

'Same,' I answer.

I don't look at Max's photo again that night. It feels as if it might bring bad luck. I pour another glass of wine, phone Tess back to tell her what's happening and fall into a dreamless sleep.

In the morning I drive to Manurewa. I park outside the court at 9.15, three-quarters of an hour early.

23

The courtroom is small. This surprises me. I'd expected something more imposing. Dominating the room is a raised platform on which stands a bench and two chairs. In front of the platform, at the lower level, is a table equipped with a computer. Sitting at this table is a bored-looking young woman with thickly gelled hair. The rest of the room is given over to rows of seats and tables, one of which is occupied by our party. The New Zealand coat of arms, hanging on the wall above the bench, and a silently ticking clock, are the only decorations.

The whanau has turned out in force. Queenie, Will, Ani, Pete, Vincent (but no Gloria; she couldn't get off work), Walter (but no Meriana; she's at home with the children), Lily (whose children are with Meriana), Lily's husband, Dave, and Ela (who has entrusted her three little ones to the care of Bethany and Albert).

We're no sooner seated than I feel a hand on my shoulder. I spin round to see Tess standing in the row behind me. I'm so happy — and surprised — to see her, I gulp back tears. We hug briefly, and I introduce her to the family. 'You should have told me,' I say to her, when we've all settled down again. 'I could have picked you up.'

'Last minute decision,' she says, grinning.

'You're the best,' I whisper.

'Actually I'm here for a purpose,' she whispers back. 'If things go the way we hope, I'll be rewriting my Saturday column.'

I take hold of her hand, and squeeze it hard. It's not the first time Tess has anticipated my wishes; only this time, she's gone further. I hadn't actually articulated, even to myself, that what I'd been praying for, for Max, was some kind of public vindication. It's typical of Tess that she should explain her decision to attend Max's inquest as a professional choice, rather than what it is, an act of love.

We don't talk after that other than in brief, whispered exchanges. Queenie keeps looking round at the No Smoking sign, as if unable to believe her eyes. Walter drums his fingers on his thighs. Lily makes strange shapes with her mouth. Will clears his throat compulsively. Ela, between yawns, fiddles with the zip on her handbag, while Vincent, uncomfortable in a tie, first loosens, then tightens it. I want to tell him to pull it off. He's not the one on trial here.

Only Ani sits impassively. And Tess, whose pale face, framed by that enviable mane of red hair, comforts me every time I look around.

'Dear God,' I pray, in an attempt to deal with my own agitation. 'Let it be all right. Let it be something we can live with. Don't punish us any more.'

'That's not the way to pray,' my mother reprimands. 'God isn't the cause of our suffering.'

'It's the only way I know,' I snap back at her.

At exactly ten o'clock the door to the side of the platform opens and a tall man in an ill-fitting suit walks in, followed by an older man with grey hair and rather better taste in clothes. The younger man — I decide he must be the clerk of the court — instructs us to 'please rise for the coroner.' When we're all seated again I find myself staring, not at the coroner, whose expression I have been unable to interpret, but at the coat of arms above his head.

The coroner clears his throat. 'In the matter of the death of Maxwell Arapata Nene,' he begins, his voice as expressionless as his face, 'my findings are as follows. After careful study of both the medical and the police evidence, much of it, I'm bound to say, contradictory, I have no alternative but to bring in a verdict which is clear as to the injury which caused Nene's death, but not as to the actual and precise circumstances in which that injury was sustained. To deal with the medical evidence first . . .'

Queenie, next to me, groans. I take her hand, and hold it tight. Glancing along the row I see we are all holding hands. A human chain of hope and grief.

I make a conscious effort to concentrate. The part of me that is fearful of the outcome wants to let my mind drift; but I know I must take in every word and register every contradiction . . . Max, we are informed, died not from his extensive internal injuries, but from a single blow to the back of the head. While I listen to the coroner's account of the pathologist's findings I see again that terrible gash — clearly visible when the body was returned to us — held together by a row of ugly stitches. That this injury was the cause of death, and not the less visible ones, comes as no surprise.

What does surprise is what the coroner has to say when he moves on to the police evidence. 'My difficulty,' he reveals, 'is in deciding exactly how Mr Nene came to suffer the fatal blow to the back of the head. In the police report, the officer who was first on the scene describes the deceased as slumped against the windscreen. This is borne out by the extensive cuts and bruises to the face detailed in the pathologist's report. Since there is no doubt as to which of Mr Nene's several injuries killed him, the position of the body cannot help but call into doubt the police assertion that Nene died in the car accident . . . In conclusion,' he finishes, 'while it is not my business to speculate, I see it as my duty to record my disquiet.'

Even while I'm telling myself this is the miracle I have been praying for, I know the word 'speculate' will be seized on by a public reluctant to have its certainties questioned. 'So what if the guy *was* dead before the car crashed?' I hear a voice argue. 'What does that prove? He was a bad bugger. Only got to look at his record.'

But the word 'miracle' persists. As it does, I suspect, glancing at the others, for all of us, with the possible exception of Ani. What we have just heard is not speculation but *vindication*.

'All rise for the coroner,' the clerk instructs.

I glance at Tess, who gives me a radiant smile. I don't need to ask her what she's thinking. She already knows what it would mean to me to see Max's name, if not cleared, then at least distanced from the worst that has been said about him.

We file out of the courtroom in a daze. 'Is that it then?' Ela asks.

Nobody answers her.

Tess, moving to stand beside me, puts a hand on my arm. 'I need to talk to you,' she says.

I glance round at the others. It's as if, I think, we're waiting for someone to tell us what to do. A soberly dressed group of people, standing about in the bright winter sunshine, unable to celebrate, in Max's absence, the possibility he was innocent. Unable, in Ani's case, even to believe in that possibility. 'It changes nothing,' she'd muttered, as we filed out.

I take Tess' hand and move her away from the family.

'Quite a turnaround,' she says, grinning at me.

'You can say that again!' I agree.

'After you phoned last night, I called Owen . . .'

I glance back at the family. The cars streaming past on the road seem to be taking their full attention. 'You remember Owen, don't you? You came to dinner with him.'

'The crime reporter? That Owen?'

'He told me the police found drugs in the car. Did you know that?'

I nod, though I hadn't known for sure. But it fits the plot I'm busy devising in my head. Roy Harawira was a drug dealer, not a deliverer of groceries.

'Heroin,' Tess goes on. 'Several wraps of it.'

Again I nod.

'Listen, I can't promise anything, but I think I can put together a convincing story . . .'

'Are you sure the *Herald* will go for it?' I ask, a sudden doubt puncturing my confidence. The *Herald* has had it in for Max ever since his first conviction. A leopard doesn't change his spots, has been the editor's view. Greg, if he were here, would agree.

'Listen,' Tess says again. 'I know what you're thinking, but you're wrong. The *Herald* will print it precisely because it's been so down on Max all this time. You know they have this policy now of admitting when they get something wrong? Well this is a perfect opportunity. If Max's injury *was* inflicted before the car crashed — and the coroner as good as said it was — it can mean only one thing. Max and Harawira fought over the drug delivery. Harawira stage-managed the accident to disguise a murder.'

I look at my friend with what I can only describe as astonished respect. I'd told her, during our abortive meeting at the café, that I couldn't believe Max sanctioned the sale of heroin to schoolchildren. To adults, maybe, but not to children. Contradictory though so much of the information about Max was, there was still no proof he had sunk to Harawira's level. I hadn't set out to convince, just to unburden myself. But Tess, thank God as things have turned out, must have taken in every word.

The story, as I'm beginning to understand it, goes like this. Max, in the wake of his fateful meeting with Income Support, threw in his lot with Harawira, believing the drugs were intended for adult use. When he discovered their true destination, he and Harawira argued. That argument ended in Max's death.

'The car wasn't stolen, you know,' Tess tells me.

'What?'

'Owen told me. You remember the police report at the time? It said they were chasing the car because it was stolen. But it wasn't.'

'How did Owen discover that?'

'He's got mates in the force. Some of them are honest.'

'So you're saying . . .'

'It was a cover-up. They were chasing the car because they knew there were drugs involved.'

'Why couldn't they have said that?'

'Because they got the wrong guy. The person they wanted was . . .'

'Roy Harawira.'

Tess nods. 'The coroner was on to it too, I'm sure of it. Only he couldn't say. Outside his brief.'

'Tess, you're amazing! Do you know that?'

'Make a damn good story, don't you think?'

We grin at each other. 'Is that why you're doing it?'

'Oh, absolutely. You know how I love stirring things up.'

I laugh. I have a strong urge to hug her. 'I suppose the police figured, if they said nothing, Harawira would think he was in the clear,' I suggest.

'And offend again,' Tess agrees. 'Exactly.'

I turn to look at the others. Pete is the only one eyeing us curiously. I wiggle my fingers at him, and turn back to Tess. 'I'll be home the rest of the day,' I tell her. 'Why don't you come over and we'll go through the whole thing together?'

'Let me get something down on paper first.'

I squeeze her arm. 'Are you always this single-minded?' I ask.

As Tess and I walk back to rejoin the family, I try to compose my features so not too many questions will be asked. I don't want to raise Queenie's hopes. And I don't want to attract Ani's scorn. Unless I'm very much mistaken, Tess is going to write a piece that will, if nothing else, sow the seeds of doubt about what Max was up to when he died. Not an absolute vindication, but an answer to the certainties of men like Greg.

'This is what I was praying for,' I remind my mother. 'If it works out, I'll let it rest. I promise.'

The phone is ringing as I walk into my flat. It had been hard to get away from Queenie. I'd had to tell her about Tess in the end, playing it down as much as possible, but emphasising how important it was that I be available to talk to her. 'Don't trust them newspaper people,' was her response.

'Tess isn't really a journalist,' I reassured her. 'She's more of a commentator . . .'

'You're as bad as Ani,' she said, dismissing my carefully understated hopes. 'Always something better to do.'

I throw down my handbag and pick up the phone. As I suspected, it's Tess. She wants to come round right away.

'Max is dead, Renate,' Ani said, during our brief exchange outside the courtroom. 'Nothing anyone says is going to bring him back.'

It was the first time since the tangi that I'd sensed her grief.

For the next fifteen minutes all I do is listen for the doorbell. When it does finally ring, I leap up from my chair as if stung by a wasp. I offer Tess coffee, but all she wants to do is read me what she's written.

'I haven't cleared it with the editor yet,' she says. 'But I've spoken to my sub, and he thinks it'll pass muster. If there's a fuss, the paper will just pass if off as the individual opinion of a starry-eyed liberal. Nothing to do with having gone soft on crime.'

'So long as it's printed,' I respond.

'Stop me if I've got anything wrong,' Tess says.

The piece is not long. Less than five hundred words is my guess. When she's finished I throw my arms round her neck. It's exactly what I'd hoped for.

'It's all right then?' Tess asks.

'It's better than all right,' I say. 'It's scrupulously fair, and that's what counts.'

I repeat my offer of coffee, but Tess is on a mission and doesn't want to be distracted. As I watch her hurry towards her car, I register, as if for the first time, the streaks of grey in her hair. In that moment I'm so filled with love for her I want to call her back and tell her what she means to me. When I first started visiting Max in prison, Tess made no secret of her anxiety about what I was doing. She didn't disapprove, she just worried about the effect prison would have on me. When I think what we've both been through since then, I can only send the words I *will* say one day chasing silently after her.

I come back into the flat, put on the disc of Beethoven's

'Ninth Symphony', pour myself a glass of wine and lie back on the sofa. I'm afraid of the things I feel — joy after so much sorrow comes freighted with disbelief.

For most of the next hour I'm aware of nothing but the music. When it ends I feel that it hasn't stopped, it has become part of me. Later, moving about the flat, touching things — my books, the broken knob of the brass bed I brought with me from England, my parent's wedding photo, the photo of Max — I feel as if I have been allowed a glimpse of another world. One in which jasmine blooms unchecked, tui shout from kowhai trees, my father walks by the river with Tolstoy, Cecil chats over a glass of bourbon with Wallace Stevens and Max argues the validity of drug-taking with Mozart. I ask myself if what I'm feeling is happiness, then realise the question is irrelevant. I don't expect to be happy again in the old way. I don't expect to love again, in the old way. But I have known happiness, and I have known love, and in that I am richly blessed. My cup, as Max would no doubt remind me, has run over many times.

I am certain of nothing, the poet John Keats wrote, *but the holiness of the heart's affections and the truth of the Imagination.*

'It's enough,' I say out loud, to Max, to Cecil, to whoever is listening. 'It's enough.'

24

The following day Tess' piece appears in the *Herald*. So far as I can make out nothing has been changed. The words are the ones Tess read to me in my flat.

Yesterday, at the coroner's court in Manurewa, doubts were raised about the police handling of the death of Maxwell Arapata Nene. Nene, according to the report published at the time, died as the result of a car crash on the southern motorway on March 30th of this year. The driver of the car, who escaped unhurt, has since been arrested in connection with another incident. He has been identified as Roy Harawira, a known drug dealer.

The coroner, Bruce McCabe, reminded the court it was not his job to speculate as to how Nene received the injury that killed him. That, he said, was a matter for the police. But he did feel obliged to draw the court's attention to the nature of the fatal injury — a blow to the back of the head. Police maintain this blow was sustained at the time of the accident. It is this assertion the coroner has called into question, pointing out that Nene was found with his head smashed against the windscreen, not thrown backwards as the injury would suggest. Mr McCabe further commented that Nene's face was badly cut and bruised, a fact that appeared to confirm his suspicion that the deceased was thrown forwards and not backwards.

Maxwell Nene, who has served three jail sentences for a variety of crimes, was released into the community in August, 1996, after serving five years for his part in the murder of a policeman. As with Nene's other convictions this offence was gang-related, and resulted in him being confined for a time in the maximum security wing of Paremoremo Prison.

During his last period in prison Nene attempted to sever his connections with the notorious Patu gang, a decision which triggered at least three attacks on him by other inmates, and may, ultimately, have been a contributing factor in his death. Roy Harawira, the driver of the car in which Nene was killed, is a known Patu associate.

Since Harawira's case is now sub judice it would be improper to speculate as to the relationship between the two men, but it is to be hoped that further light will be shed at Harawira's trial.

It has been said that Maxwell Nene died while on a drug run. He has been accused of involvement in a ring that sold drugs to schoolchildren. But Nene is not here to defend himself. Justice demands that questions be asked. For the sake of his family, who were at the coroner's court in considerable numbers, it is to be hoped answers will be found.

All that day my phone doesn't stop ringing: Queenie, Pete, my mother, Tess, Walter, Lily . . . I am reminded of the day Cecil died. Then I could speak to no one. Now I want to speak to the whole world. I'm even tempted to phone Greg. Something in me still wants to share things with him. When I think of how astonished, and then enraged, he would be, I smile. Just because one part of my life has been touched by a miracle doesn't mean the whole has been transformed.

'I don't think I want to wait till the weekend,' I say to Pete. 'Why don't we visit the grave tomorrow? All of us.'

When he doesn't answer I suspect I've blundered, but then I hear him blow his nose, and realise he's fighting back tears. 'I'll arrange it,' he says.

'Why should Harawira tell the truth?' Ani carps, when, later in the day, I get to speak to her. 'It won't help *him* any.'

'It doesn't matter,' I answer her. I'm tired suddenly. It's been a long day. And Ani's scepticism is not what I want to hear. 'We've made people doubt, *that's* what matters.'

'Harawira's just as likely to dob Max in. Make *him* out to be the ringleader.'

'And you think a jury will believe him?'

Ani sighs. 'You don't give up, Renate, do you?'

The last thing I do before I go to bed is ring Daphne. I hadn't forgotten her. Other things just got in the way.

'You're sure, love?' she says, when I urge her to come and stay as long as she likes. 'I won't be in the way?'

'You never know,' I answer her. 'I might decide to come back with you.'

Next morning I wake early. My bedroom is filled with a lemony light. The tui shouts from his perch amongst the blossoming kowhai. I listen to the train rumbling over the rails and picture the early commuters, their noses pressed to the windows, their spirits lifted by the promise of warmth in the misty sunlight.

I make coffee and toast and eat it on the balcony. The sight of the jasmine rioting through the hedge makes me laugh out loud. The arrangement is that I'll pick up Ela and the children at 10.30, leaving Queenie and Will to travel separately with Rewi. We'll then join Pete and the others at 11, at the cemetery.

I glance at my watch — 7.30 — far too early to take to the road. On the other hand, if I leave now, I can take my time, detour if I feel like it, think about the novel.

The casino tower is coloured green today, the colour of hope. Last week it was blue. Someone has forgotten to switch off the lights. By this time of day the tower should be the colour of steel.

Half an hour later I'm in my car, cruising down the southern motorway. I've experimented with twenty different opening sentences. That none of them sound right doesn't worry me. The voice will come when it's ready.

I'm about to take the turn-off to Queenie's when the words come. Or rather, not so much the words as the image needed to start the story. I pull over on to the hard shoulder and take out my notebook.

The girl was a stranger, I write. *A frail, bird-like creature, her hair trailing damply over the coffin, her body wracked with sobs. Not one of us in that room knew her name . . .*

199

By the time I get to Queenie's I've written a couple of hundred words and there are a couple of hundred more backed up in my head.

Queenie comes to the door herself, embraces me warmly and leads me into the lounge. 'You can take that look off your face right now,' she says to Rewi, continuing a conversation my arrival clearly interrupted. 'You ride with your father in his car. I'm not having any more members of my family killed . . . Motorbike,' she explains, when Rewi has left the room. 'Some fool kid has left his here for my grandson to take care of. I ask you . . .'

'You're looking wonderful today, Queenie,' I say. And she is. Her hair is done up on top of her head, adding to her already considerable height. She is wearing a long black skirt with a silky cream blouse and her customary red and green shawl.

'You don't look too bad yourself,' she says, grinning at me.

There follows a confused domestic time while we gather up Ela's children, tie up the dogs in the back yard and call out to the neighbours, who have come out of their houses to wish us well. Will, sidling up to me on the porch, remarks that as we're not going to a wedding, and we're not going to a funeral, what we're going to must have a name all of its own.

'A celebration?' I suggest.

He smiles. 'To listen to Queenie you'd think Max had been given a royal pardon,' he confides.

My car, with Ela and her five children as passengers, is the first to get away. We follow the route taken by Max on his last earthly journey and arrive, fifteen minutes later, at the cemetery.

'Where is everyone?' Ela asks, looking round irritably.

'We're early,' I reassure her.

The mist has lifted, allowing the sun to shine cleanly on this place of sorrows. I look at the mountain first (*I will lift up mine eyes unto the hills, from whence cometh my help*), at its uneven terraces, and lone Norfolk pine. Then I lower my gaze to the level of the stone church, with its border of flowering hibiscus. Max was buried in the autumn when the hibiscus blooms were curling and browning at the edges. Now, though it's still officially winter, the trees are covered in bright pink and red flowers.

Here and there, amongst the headstones, mourners sit talking to their dead, or silently meditating, while others busy themselves gardening, pulling out weeds and arranging flowers in glass jars. A couple of children, too young for school, play amongst the headstones. Their squeals of delight provoke an outburst from Ela's children. 'Can't we get out?' Bethany complains from the back seat. 'It's squashed in here.'

'You'll do as you're told,' Ela growls.

'Billy's pissed himself,' Bethany announces a moment later. She sounds triumphant, as if that was exactly what she wanted her little brother to do.

'Billy's always pissing himself,' Ela replies calmly.

Eventually the others turn up and we form a ragged group on the grass at the edge of the cemetery. Apart from Paea, all the immediate family is present. Gloria cheerfully confesses to having phoned in sick, while Meriana, whom I hadn't expected to see, stands with one arm around Rewi, smiling vaguely.

As we set out towards Max's grave I find myself walking between Lily and Walter. Lily curls her hand through my arm. Her other hand is occupied holding her youngest child.

There is no shape to our party. We are bunched together like a flock of sheep, shuffling our way towards new pasture. No one has told the children to keep quiet, but they do. Even the babies are silent.

I think of the day of Max's burial, of the men standing at the top of the bank we are now climbing, chanting their ancient song of sorrow and loss. I think of the old woman and her echoing karanga and Queenie's unquenchable grief. I try not to think too vividly of Max, though that is what we are here for. Ani's right. Max may be vindicated, but that hasn't brought him back to life.

Halfway up the bank we pause and Will, who has been walking at the front with Queenie, turns round and offers us each a hibiscus bloom. I hadn't noticed he was carrying flowers. If Max had been here he would have stolen those flowers from the over-burdened trees by the church. But Will won't have stolen them. He'll have picked them from the tree growing in Queenie's yard.

I watch Will move round the group, smiling, chucking chins, whispering encouragement. When he reaches me he doesn't say anything, but his eyes are eloquent. Then he goes back to his wife, takes her arm, and the disordered procession, led by a limping Queenie, continues.

Max's grave is marked by a simple cross. A headstone, and words, will come later, but for now the cross is all we have. There is even a moment when we wonder if we have the right grave. But Pete reassures us. He has been a regular visitor.

Queenie is the first to place her flower by the cross. She bends down, kisses the ground, and speaks some words in Maori, which I am too far off to catch.

Ani, eldest of her children now, goes next. She too speaks in Maori, but so softly I doubt anyone hears.

Next comes Walter. His words are plain and to the point. 'So long, bro,' he says. 'Keep out of trouble from now on, eh? Miss you. Miss you heaps.'

Meriana follows; then her children, each in turn placing a flower on the grave. Rewi is the only one of Walter's children to speak. 'Why did you have to die, Uncle Max?' he mutters. 'You an' me, we were mates. Why did you have to die?'

Vincent and Gloria step forward together, Vincent, to my astonishment, lifting his arm in what looks suspiciously like a military salute.

Finally it's my turn. I'm the last to go, after Pete. There is no reason for this. It's just how it turns out. I put my flower with the others and try to say goodbye, but the word sticks in my throat. 'I hope you're getting sorted,' I say instead. Which makes Ela, standing behind me, giggle.

A few minutes later we're straggling down the bank, the children noisy now the ceremony is over. 'Don't forget to wash your hands,' Walter yells.

The older children rush for the tap at which everyone must

wash before leaving the burial ground. Queenie and Will wait till last, queuing patiently behind their children and grandchildren, their arms linked, their faces tilted upwards as if to greet the sun.

We go back to the house, to food and beer; to talking and laughter and singing. As I listen to the flow of conversation, to the occasional cross word as a parent argues with a child, and the occasional tears as an over-tired baby is hustled off to bed, words from the novel begin to flow through my head, a river of words with no beginning and no end. I panic that I might forget them, then tell myself to relax. A river can't be lost; the worst that can happen is that it goes underground.

It's nearly midnight when I finally make it back to my flat. Queenie wanted me to stay, but I knew that if I slept the river would disappear and I would have to dig for days to find it again.

I open the door and literally run to my desk. The world beyond my window is silent, the tower flashing noiselessly above the sleeping city.

I bring up a new file, title it *Loving Max*, and transfer the words from my notebook to the screen. More words follow, not a river but a torrent. *Chapter One* I write; then, two hours later, *Chapter Two*. I know much of what I write will go into the trash. I'll be lucky if a few hundred words survive. But the voice is still clear in my head. As clear as the voices of my unseen companions.

By the time I've finished, the first signs of daylight have appeared on the horizon. I go through to my bedroom, throw off my clothes, think about having a shower, but fall into the bed instead. My eyes close; then, suddenly, open again. Something about the room is different. It's not the light, creeping in behind the drawn curtains. Nor is it the bed with its reminders of other rooms and other countries. It's something else. Something small and shining my eye registered earlier, but failed to identify.

Fighting off sleep I force myself to examine, from my semi-prone position, the contents of my bedroom. My clothes are a heap on the chair. *They* are not the cause of my wakefulness.

The wardrobe is closed. No explanation there. The chest of drawers is covered with its usual tangle of discarded earrings and scarves and make-up. Next to it, underneath the mirror, is another chair on which sits a handbag and a pair of sunglasses.

That only leaves my beside table. I sit up. See through tired eyes the pile of books, the alarm clock, my occasionally required reading glasses and last night's glass of water.

'I must have dreamt it,' I say out loud.

And then I see it, twinkling modestly from behind the pile of books. A thin gold band encrusted with seed pearls. Cecil's ring.

I turn my head abruptly, fearing that what I am looking at is a chimera, a product of my overwrought imagination. But when I turn back the ring is still there. I reach out to touch it. It's real all right. The tiny pearls are tiny bumps under my fingertips.

I pick it up and slip it on my finger. There was never any question which finger it would go on. 'Is it finished?' I whisper into the empty room.

'It's only just beginning,' is the answer I get.

But whose voice that answer came in, is my secret.